HEAVEN HELP
HELEN SLOANE

Also by J. R. Lucas

Seriously Funny (Adrian Plass with Jeff Lucas)

Lucas Unleashed

I Was Just Wandering

Grace Choices

HEAVEN HELP
HELEN SLOANE

a Novel

J.R. LUCAS

ZONDERVAN®

ZONDERVAN.com/
AUTHORTRACKER
follow your favorite authors

ZONDERVAN

Heaven Help Helen Sloane
Copyright © 2012 by Jeff Lucas

This book was previously published in the UK by Authentic Media, 2008, under the title *Helen Sloane's Diary.*

This title is also available as a Zondervan ebook.
Visit www.zondervan.com/ebooks.

This title is also available in a Zondervan audio edition.
Visit www.zondervan.fm.

Requests for information should be addressed to:

Zondervan, *Grand Rapids, Michigan 49530*

Library of Congress Cataloging-in-Publication Data

Lucas, Jeff, 1956 –
    Heaven help Helen Sloane : a novel / Jeff Lucas.
      p.   cm.
    ISBN 978-0-310-28152-8 (softcover)
    1. Women social workers — Fiction. 2. Burn out (Psychology) — Fiction.
  3. England — Social conditions — Fiction. 4. Diary fiction. I. Title.
  PS3612.U2364H43 2011
  813'.6 — dc22
2011043695

Cover design: ThinkPen Design
Cover photography: Getty Images, Dan Hallman
Interior design: Beth Shagene

Printed in the United States of America

---

12 13 14 15 16 17 18 /DCI/ 20 19 18 17 16 15 14 13 12 11 10 9 8 7 6 5 4 3 2 1

To Dinah and Stuart:

Thanks so much
for the years of wonderful friendship:
with much love

HEAVEN HELP
HELEN SLOANE

Great. I've begun. Here goes.

I, Helen Sloane, have now joined the ranks of the thoughtful literati who keep a journal. In the pages that follow I shall chronicle (hopefully with winsome wit and flair) the hopes, dreams, fears, successes, and failures that unfold in the coming year. Who knows what stunning riches of wisdom might flow from my two-fingered typing as I reflect here upon my journey? Great trees grow out of tiny acorns ...

Tonight I'm totally exhausted from my first day back at work after the Christmas break, so the odds are against me writing anything that might win a Nobel Prize for literature. Perhaps tomorrow.

Life as a newly qualified social worker (two months in the job, working on the Children's Services Team) is demanding. The holiday break already seems like ancient history. Tonight my head's buzzing with client updates, court papers, chatter from today's team strategy meeting, and what seems like an entire filing cabinet of case notes.

Add to this my role as a small-group leader in Frenton-on-Sea's New Wave Christian Fellowship (someone obviously thought that the "new wave" maritime play on words was a bright idea), plus the demands of my busy social calendar, and the result is a frantic life navigated at high speed. I hardly have time to breathe, never mind think, pray, or reflect.

Hence this diary. I've thought about keeping a diary/journal before, but the notion seemed vaguely antique, the kind of activity that Edwardian English women would engage in (alongside needlepoint and yelling at servants). I am an Englishwoman living in England; I tried needlepoint once and nearly bled to death, and it goes without saying that I am somewhat short of servants. Nevertheless, a diary I shall keep.

The diary idea came from my mildly kooky best friend Vanessa, who came up with the idea last Saturday during our New Year's Day lunch together. Vanessa.

Vee is beautiful. The quintessential Californian girl, Vee is blessed with bouncy long blond hair, soaring cheekbones, and impossibly aqua-blue eyes. She is utterly gorgeous, and quite unaware of it, which makes her even lovelier. Her skin seems to tan at the slightest hint of sun, which is helpful for an American like her living in England, where sunshine is usually just that—a hint. She has perfect legs that seem to stretch into eternity. And speaking of the eternal, she is one of the few females on earth who makes a black T-shirt (with the words Rapture Ready emblazoned across it in silver lettering) actually look good.

Vanessa also is blessed with teeth to die for. They are brilliant white, and perfectly straight, like piano keys.

I'm glad that Vanessa's beauty doesn't intimidate me. Despite my being two sizes larger than she is, and even though she is stunning in her tight black jeans and scarlet leather jacket over that black T-shirt (charity store treasures that look a million dollars on Vee), I always feel comfortable about how I look when we're together.

Vee came to Frenton five years ago as part of a short-term youth mission team that was sent over from California. She decided to stay. Or, as she so simply put it, "God commanded her to put down firm roots in this ancient nation and help re-dig the wells of the Spirit that have been blocked by unbelief since the Saxons." She works in Frenton's trendiest fashion store, Cats, and says that her getting a British employment visa was nothing short of a miracle and is "confirmation that she is surely experiencing the favor and anointing of God." (Am not sure how she's doing at unblocking the unbelieving wells, but her beauty and trendy Californian accent certainly help her to consistently be salesperson of the month at Cats.)

I'm really not sure what those naughty Saxons did to constipate the spiritual wells of the land, but I'm really glad that Vee stayed. And it would surely have taken a direct order from God to inspire anyone to exchange the golden beaches and shimmering blue skies of San Diego for the bleak promenade of oh-so-English Frenton. Anyway, we've become very close, Vee and me. Her kindness eclipses her weirdness, which means she is very kind indeed. And she does make me laugh a lot—sometimes with her, sometimes at her.

Vanessa goes to the big happening church in town, Infusion, which has a high-energy worship team and an age demographic of about twelve. I have been tempted to go there myself, but the band seems to be on Duracells, and I don't think I could maintain that level of consistent ecstasy. I love to worship, and the calorie burn that would result from all the flag waving and worship dancing would be beneficial, but right now I don't have any spare energy.

So, on Saturday we were having lunch in Marinabean, our coffee shop of choice—mainly because it's Frenton-on-Sea's only decent coffee shop, Frenton being a tad behind in the designer-caffeine craze. We have a few rather homely seafront cafés that serve lots of steaming cups of tea to pensioners, but they also turn out horrid instant coffee that tastes like Brazilian mud. Hence our patronage of Marinabean.

Marinabean is comfortable, but not plush. An exhausted leather sofa languishes in the corner, torn and tarnished by too many bored, smoothie-sipping teenagers. Colorful posters of coffee beans caught spilling out of branded sacks adorn the vanilla walls. A huge Italian espresso machine, which looks like a shiny brass steam engine, dominates a marble countertop. Moist pastries and muffins line up in a glass display, manna from heaven, temptation from hell. It's homey, and a little incongruous; Seattle comes to Frenton, but not quite.

The place was hopping, but we bagged the round smoked-glass table we call "ours" in the window bay, ideal for the delicious sport of people watching. Elderly Elton John droned on, too loudly, insisting that Saturday night is all right for fighting. As usual, we asked the rather overweight, pimply teenager who sports a Barry the Barista badge to turn the music down. As usual, he agreed, and then didn't. We didn't mind too much.

We chattered on about nothing much for a while, and then Vee flashed her "I wanna get spiritual" expression that warned me that we were now moving on to more profound issues.

"So, Helen, mate, what are your hopes for the coming year?"

I always wince just a little when she says "mate." It's a habit she's picked up over the years that she's been in England, in a kind of I-can-talk-like-a-native way, but it sounds odd, forced. It's like the English saying "Have a nice day" when they return from a vacation in Florida; it sounds wrong somehow.

I glanced out the window, and as is usual for Frenton, it was raining hard. Beads of water clung to the cloudy glass, and reluctant shoppers hurried by, hunched against the cold, eager to get their stuff and get home. I looked down into my coffee cup for inspiration, desperate to say something weighty and profound.

Vanessa didn't wait for me to answer. "I just know we're going to see great things. I'm determined to do something that makes a difference—something with a clear impact. I want demons to tremble and angels to dance." Just the thought of such exciting happenings made her grin and wiggle. "What about you?"

"Hmmm ... I guess I do want to try to get fit. Lose a few pounds—say fifteen. Just enough to get fit and thin. Not waiflike à la Keira Knightley—she probably only eats once a month—but just enough to enable me to be rescued from a blazing inferno by a gorgeous fireman without giving him a double hernia." I waggled my eyebrows in appreciation of the thought.

Vee rolled her eyes. "Jesus never owned a treadmill, and John the Baptist—he who prepared the way of the Lord—didn't do Atkins."

Vital information, although I was tempted to comment about all that low-carb snacking on locusts and wild honey. Instead I stirred my cappuccino, as if some clever words about the year to come might suddenly appear in the froth. For some reason, I remembered Jim Carrey in *Bruce Almighty* parting his soup, Red Sea style, and fantasized for a moment about performing a miracle with the froth. And then, for a weird nanosecond, I fantasized about Jim Carrey. Vanessa nudged me.

"It's good to want to lose a little weight, Helen, but God wants you to grow spiritually this year. And spiritual growth comes from considered reflection. Saint Simeon Stylites, the ancient ascetic, sat on top of a pole for many years in complete solitude, covered in sores and crusted in his own filth. His only contact with the rest of the world was a bucket used for receiving food and disposing of his … well, you know. But I bet that man knew himself and knew his God."

I thought that rancid old Simeon probably didn't know anyone else apart from himself and God, what with those hygiene habits, but I said nothing. I quietly decided that poop buckets and parking on poles would not play any part in my life this year and then realized with a pang of yet more guilt that I'm useless at discipline of any kind.

Vanessa started talking about a book on spiritual discipline that she's been reading. "It's completely fantastic, Helen. It's really fueled my prayer life. And I can't wait to get into a more regular habit of fasting."

I've read the same book, and it just made me feel like an utter failure, worthy of wearing a sackcloth miniskirt and a pile of ashes on my head. Like many Christians, I'm really, really good at feeling really, really guilty, which means that something is amiss, seeing as the gospel is supposed to be good news. Sometimes my knees buckle under the tyranny of Christian oughts. I ought to pray more, ought to give more, care more, love more ...

Life without so many oughts occasionally sounds rather delicious.

And abstaining from food is never going to be something that I look forward to. I stifled the uncomfortable thought that there are moments when I wish I had never become a Christian in the first place. Life without faith might be pointless, but it would, perhaps, be less complicated. Pointlessness can sound quite attractive, at least as a temporary condition. This thought lands in my brain every now and again, more a feeling than a stream of logic, and I mentally swat it like a pesky mosquito. I feel guilty for even writing it down now.

Anyway, I instinctively bristle at the use of the word *spiritual*, as in *spiritual disciplines*. I don't think that we should chop our lives up into sacred and secular slices. Surely God is interested in all of our lives—our bodies, fun, leisure, work, and relationships—not just the bit that we mistakenly designate as holy or spiritual. But I didn't say any of this. I listened as Vee put her hand on my arm and urged me towards austerity.

"Helen, can you remember the last time God clearly answered one of your prayers?"

"Uh ..." I racked my brains for a second or two. "Nothing comes to mind. I know, maybe I should pray for a better memory, and then, when I get it, I'd remember to be grateful."

It was then that Vanessa said she was convinced that a journal would help my amnesiac tendencies. Her advice was blunt: "Make a commitment, Helen. Write stuff down every day."

Her idea clicked with me immediately because I've got a good feeling about this year and I don't want to miss a moment. Plus a daily appointment with my laptop beats buckets and poles hands down.

It's just the discipline thing that's the challenge.

Vanessa stirred her drink and took a sip. "I've been praying a lot. And I'm positive good things are coming. This will be the year of breakthrough."

"The year of breakthrough." Sounds very nice. I have to be honest, though—call me Thomas if you like (the doubting disciple, not the train)—I'm not sure about the way Vanessa gives each year a spiritual tag. We've been friends for ages, so over the last few years she's made a few predictions, and I'm not convinced that they've been fulfilled. Last year was supposed to be the "year of harvest" and the one before that was the "year of an open heaven," which followed the "year of refreshing." Maybe she's right, but all this sounds a bit Chinese to me ("year of the rat" and all that) and I can't honestly say that we've seen too much spiritual harvest or notable refreshing in Frenton-on-Sea. And the only open heaven we experienced two years ago was a record rainfall in August. The deluge washed half the beach away and left piles of stinking seaweed, which I don't think was much of a blessing, unless you're into do-it-yourself seaweed spa wraps.

Vanessa was on a roll. "The year of breakthrough. God is going to do something in Frenton that will reverberate around the nations and traumatize the very powers of hell."

I do love her, but it's unlikely that our rather grey little town with half a windswept pier is going to become the epicenter of God's purposes for Planet Earth.

I feel guilty for questioning Vanessa's enthusiasm. And yet, when does asking questions about this stuff become cynicism? When does not asking questions become sheer stupidity? I can't help thinking that questions help us toward a more realistic, mature faith. So why does asking them make me feel so guilty?

I suddenly realized that two of my very favorite people —Vanessa and my mother—are both quite odd when it comes to spiritual issues, but for totally different reasons. I wondered if this is why I feel confused about faith so much of the time.

Vanessa paused for a breath, and I jumped in. "Okay, then, here's something: this year I am going to follow a 'Read through the entire Bible in one year' course. In fact I've already started—this morning I read Genesis chapters 1 through 4." I looked at her triumphantly and refrained from adding that I'd read it all in thirty-seven seconds. Perhaps I should do a "Read through the entire Bible in forty-five minutes even if you take a five-minute coffee break" course instead.

Vanessa decided to end our lunch with a peppy word of encouragement. "Grab the moment, Helen. Make some good decisions about how your life will be. Carpe diem, and all that. The hour is late. We're surely in the end times."

I do find her Second Coming theories as excruciating as chalk being scraped on a blackboard. Not wanting to get into a lengthy conversation about Israel and temples being rebuilt and the signs of the times, I used one of my proven techniques, and changed the conversation with a shocking statement. It's the verbal equivalent of grabbing the steering wheel and pointing the car down a side street.

"I know what I want this year, Vee. I want a man. And I want sex."

Well I think that's it for today. I am feeling rather happy to have completed my first diary entry. A good start. I'm excited about the unswerving discipline that I'll employ to record my thoughts every day without fail, absolutely. I vow it solemnly to God, mark my words, so be it.

Lord, here's my year. Stay close. Amen.

Woke up feeling very slightly irritated. I love Vanessa, but our conversation didn't end so well. My moment of brutal honesty about men and sex prompted Vanessa to give me a short, kind, and completely unnecessary little talking to about sex outside of marriage, which was caring and pointless. I've given the same talk to others many times, so I know the script. I wish that Christians would sometimes avoid the temptation to fix everything and everybody; perhaps we'd be a little more honest with each other if we felt that a little raw self-disclosure wouldn't be instantly countered with well-meaning advice.

Besides, I don't want to be immoral, just intimate.

I want to have sex, preferably while I am still young enough to experience it without dying during the process. My confession to Vee makes me feel like Helen "the scarlet woman/brazen hussy" Sloane, fit only to hang out with Rahab the harlot, or even that Jezebel who was snacked on by dogs. But actually that's not the way it is.

I do want sex as a married person. Which means that, yes, of course, I want to hear wedding bells. But I need to own up to the fact that I frantically want to cuddle as well as walk the aisle. And I would like God to know that I think I'll spontaneously combust if this doesn't happen soon. It's better to marry than burn, say the Scriptures, and right now a quick emergency call to bring out the fire department would be in order—not least because it would cause a few muscle-bound firemen to beat a pathway to my door ...

Felt just a little blue on the way to work.

My flat is in a side street just off the boardwalk, and I always drive down the prom to get to work, mainly so I can look at the ocean for a few moments. I glanced out at the cold sea; it is a sight that usually cheers — I love the water — but today it nudged me towards gloom. Frenton's seafront is more like a quarry than a beach. A hundred-yard-wide blanket of pebbles edges the shore, only surrendering to muddy wet sand at low tide. A broken neon sign on the Fish and Chip shop advertises "Fis_ and _hips." I drove past the broken pier; the big storm of 1979 amputated it, cutting it in half and sweeping a rather tacky amusement arcade out to sea. Now the pier is a busted construction that goes nowhere. There's no money or inclination to rebuild it, or demolish it. It just is.

I suddenly felt a rush of panic. Frenton is tired. Even when the seafront is decorated with lights for Christmas, it still seems like an unsuccessful makeover on a very ugly woman. Is that me? Will I, like Frenton, just trundle on, more of the same, too many days filed away in the "not much happened" folder?

Thursday, January 6

Looking at my diary entry of yesterday, and surprised that I felt so gloomy. Am so glad that getting into work, sharing a quick coffee with Laura, our lovely receptionist, and generally putting my head down and getting on with a busy day made me feel so much better. Am hoping that keeping a journal is not going to make me introspective in a negative way. Good to realize that a mood doesn't have to last all day—or all year.

Vanessa called to ask how my journaling is going. Was delighted to tell her I have been doing rather well. She's coming round tonight—we're going to rent the latest George Clooney. What a fine actor he is. He really should become a Christian and marry me immediately. Vee loves to watch American films—she says they remind her of home. But then she always feels a hankering for Mexican food, which apparently is wonderful in the USA—and nonexistent in Frenton. And so Vee and I always end the evening by making the best chicken fajitas in the whole of England. Mmm. Fasting can wait.

Tuesday, January 11

7:15 p.m.

Can't believe that five days have gone by and I completely forgot that I am now committed to keeping a journal. Note to self: must do better. Not a great display of discipline —and obviously no answer to prayer yet about getting a better memory. Have now decided to go on a forty-day fast to create a slimmer, more godly me, as well as giving me a nifty detox. I did go to the gym today, which was awful, and not only because of the excruciating torment inflicted by those evil weight-training machines that were probably in use during the Spanish Inquisition, alongside the rack. The pain came from the irritating presence of old Mrs. Hemming from church. Don't mean to be ageist here; we've got some totally wonderful elderly people in our church, but Mrs. Hemming definitely isn't one of them. I don't think her problem has anything to do with age, though. She has probably been practicing being unpleasant from a very early age and now has it down to a fine art.

She goes to the gym once each month to do her two-miles-per-hour walk/crawl on the treadmill and, as she says to anyone who'll listen, "to be salt and light in the community and reach out to the lost."

Today she reported on yet another evangelistic triumph:

"I've noticed, Helen, that Colin, that young instructor who wears disgracefully tight shorts, is now avoiding me completely. Every time I walk into the gym, he heads for the office area immediately. I did have a rather providential conversation with him a few weeks ago, during which I was able to share with him that his current lifestyle is going to take him straight to hell. I'm convinced he's avoiding me because he's feeling convicted. God is at work in his life, mark my words, Helen. When we're truly salt, marvelous things happen."

She's certainly like salt, or at least the feeling of salt when it's rubbed into a wound. And as for being a light, she certainly stands out from the crowd, but that's because she's tortoise slow; it's like watching a waxwork in a leotard. She always wears her fluorescent multicolored

Lycra all-in-one outfit that was probably highly fashionable when Noah was into floating zoos.

Worst of all, today she wouldn't shut up while I was sweating my way through my workout. She followed me around the gym, parked herself on whatever machine was next to mine and blathered on. She must have muscles of iron—in her jaws.

It is strange seeing someone like Mrs. Hemming in a gym—like bumping into the pope in a bar. She just doesn't look the part.

Despite the gym being a temple of physical exertion, her short silver hair was, as usual, perfectly in place. I want to touch her hair (and so *don't* want to touch her hair), because I feel the same fascination for her hairstyle that one might feel for an odd-looking animal in the zoo. I think she uses too much hair spray, what sits on her scalp is more a hardened crust than a head of hair.

She carries a huge bosom, which, if not restrained, could be a danger to other exercisers should she actually exert herself greatly. Which is unlikely. She does not walk or run on the treadmill. She marches, like a vengeful crusader on the hunt for infidels. A very slow march, which would mean that the infidels would be quite safe.

Today she stumbled off the treadmill, forgetting to press the red Stop button. I am worried by the joy that her momentary pain brought me. She scowled at the machine, as if it were responsible for stopping itself. Mrs. Hemming is very good at scowling; her face seems locked into a permanent frown. Nothing this side of the grave seems to be able to budge it. When she dies, and no longer has any muscular control, the skin of her face surely will fall quite naturally into a scowl that will only ultimately be wiped away by decomposition.

I know that we Christians are supposed to love absolutely everybody with the exception of the devil, but Mrs. Hemming is so incredibly unlikable, and she is married to Mr. Hemming (I don't know if either one of them actually has a first name), and I don't like him either. He's the senior deacon in our church, which means that (a) he knows loads of the Bible and quotes it endlessly—usually out of context. And (b) he's seen about eleven ministers come and go and yet, however good they are, he gives the impression that he's really the one in charge. Even though he's loud and rude, most people in the church are afraid of him and rarely challenge what he says and does. (The only person he seems to be afraid of is his wife.) Also, some of us live with a niggling worry that we do need to respect our leaders even if they're obnoxious, so we don't like to take him on. Vanessa is always banging on about making sure we bless and honor our leaders, whatever they're like. Another tricky one to think through . . .

Having recovered from her stumble off of the treadmill, Mrs. H. walked over to the elliptical machine where I was feeling very close to death. In my head, I heard the ominous shark music from Jaws.

"Hello again, dear," she hissed. Mrs. Hemming has the ability to make even the kindest statement sound slightly acidic. I think that she could even make the wondrous words "I love you" sound like a bit of a talking to.

I pretended to not hear, and even hummed along to

the music in my iPod, and then realized that I didn't have my earphones in. She was unperturbed. Mrs. Hemming doesn't need a response in order to have a lengthy conversation that is, in fact, a monologue. If talking was an Olympic sport, then Mrs. Hemming would get a gold medal every four years, that's for sure, and today I felt like blessing her with a slap; she's such a gossip. She says she loves to "share" and manages to whisper scandalous rumors about people under the guise that she is passing on prayer requests.

"We need to know what's happening, Helen, dear," she hissed as I fought the urge to die during my fourth set of reps on the bench press, "so that we can pray more faithfully and accurately."

She then told me about one of the deacons whose teenage daughter apparently smoked dope at a New Year's Eve party.

"I'm shocked to say that it's been rumored that this girl smoked some kind of illegal substance while participating in the ungodly revelry," Mrs. Hemming whispered conspiratorially. "We need to pray that that wretched girl will see some sense and come to true, heartfelt repentance," she said. "And also that God will give the diaconate wisdom to know if her father is still biblically qualified to serve in leadership, what with him having such a disgustingly wayward child ..."

Totally disagree with her notion that someone is disqualified to lead because of the behavior of their adult children and long to shove her face into some of my case notes to show her what the real world is like, but I need all available oxygen for the challenging task of breathing. I just grunted, which I think she thought meant that I was agreeing. Her believing she could be mistaken is as likely as a bacon sandwich at a bar mitzvah.

Anyway, she blathered on about deficient parenting (she's an expert, although, as far as I know, she's never had children), and prayer ("I try to give at least an hour a day to intercession, dear"), and the general infestation of the gym by utter pagans ("I look at them working so hard on their bodies and think, 'But what of your souls, you lost fools?'"), and as I huffed and puffed I wondered if God himself ever gets bored senseless by Mrs. Hemming's daily prayer activity. I thought of that story in the Bible —I think it's called the parable of the importunate widow —when a woman keeps on knocking at a door until she gets her request. If Mrs. Hemming was at my door and I was God, I'd give her anything she asked for after the first knock.

After ten agonizing minutes, I excused myself and headed for the sauna, knowing that Mrs. Hemming would not follow me there, because it involves nakedness. Even though the sauna is for females only, Mrs. Hemming still worries that it could be an opportunity for lascivious carnality.

I sweated alone in the pine box and realized that Mrs. Hemming's grating monologue had slightly depressed me and given me a tinge of a hopeless "what's the point in bothering with discipline if being spiritual might transform me into being a tiresome old bat" feeling. I swatted that mosquito away.

Later, coming out of the changing room, I spotted Mrs. Hemming in the reception area. She was complaining to one of the personal trainers about the "malfunctioning" treadmill that "very nearly gave me a very serious injury." I fled the gym, lest I be called as a witness.

I'm starving. Forty-day fast starting to bite now. No pain, no gain. I'm pushing through.

9:00 p.m.

I have decided to bring the forty-day fast to an end as I am nervous about anorexia, malnutrition, and other issues that might lead to an untimely death. Besides, I'm in negative caloric balance due to all that wickedly demanding gym activity today, plus the nervous tension exerted listening to Mrs. Hemming's time of sharing. Unfortunately I ordered Chinese takeout and followed it up with some of Ben & Jerry's finest.

Dad called to see how my work week was going.

"Hello, love. How are things? Not getting overwhelmed, are you?"

Dad worries that I'll struggle to deal with the emotional weight of my career choice. He's a quiet, thoughtful type —the most fabulous listener I've ever met. Despite the fact that he's a man of few words, I'm certain about two things: he utterly worships my mother, even though they're so different, and his view of me is wonderfully close to adulation, which of course I like a lot.

"I'm fine, Dad. Better than fine, actually. I'm on a fitness kick! Well, somewhat of a kick. A nudge, perhaps." I told him about my forty-day fast that had turned into a twelve-hour fast.

Dad voiced the usual encouragements. "Well, to be honest, I'm relieved. Helen, darling, with the warp speed of your life, you need nourishment."

"This from Mr. High Velocity 'I'm supposed to be retired but have instead joined Frenton-on-Sea Town Council.'"

"Well, you know the saying: 'Do as I say ...'"

With that rousing encouragement, he put Mum on the phone.

"Darling, listen to your father. He knows what he's talking about. Of course, it never hurts to try to better yourself." And with that she launched into details of her new adzuki-bean mango bran diet, which sounded like a sure recipe for a gastric tropical storm.

Time for bed.

Wednesday, January 12

My Bible reading today was in Genesis 6, about the Flood. Reading the story again brought back memories of my schooldays, when we had a Christian youth worker visit our school and he did a question-and-answer session. Someone went on the attack and asked him why God did something so horrific as to flood the earth. The poor lad looked completely lost, and there was a long silence. Finally he spluttered, "I have no idea why God did that, but he did promise that he'd never ever do it again." Smiled at the memory but wondered again why God did that . . .

Had lunch with Laura at a pizza place: lovely extra-thick stuffed-crust, Canadian bacon, and pineapple—perhaps made slightly healthy by the bits of iceberg lettuce on top—followed by Banoffee Pie. And cream. And a chocolate mint and a latte to finish.

The main thing that happened today is that my small group from church didn't happen tonight, which I quite liked. I love the group, and it's fairly easy co-leading it with my friend James, but when I found out that two or three of the group are either away or struggling with the sniffly cold thing that's going around (which Vanessa says we warriors of faith should be impervious to), we decided to cancel the evening and I stayed home and watched TV. Nice.

Friday, January 14

Once again I've missed another couple of days of journaling and defaulted on my Bible-reading plan too. This discipline stuff isn't as easy as I thought. But I have had my first attempt at the Tropical Storm diet, which meant that most of the day was spent seated . . .

I had coffee with Vanessa after work tonight and told her about my lingering irritation/temptation toward inflicting grievous bodily harm on the grievous busybody that is Mrs. Hemming.

"Well, it's not Mrs. Hemming who's the problem. It's Satan." Vee affirmed.

Had a terrible thought: that sometimes Mrs. Hemming and the Prince of Darkness share very similar behavioral patterns. Is Mrs. Hemming actually Satan incarnate?

"Perhaps you're just going through a period of spiritual warfare." Rather than depress her, as it did me, Vee was excited. "You must be doing something right, Helen," she insisted, presumably to cheer me up.

"So you're saying that the advent of tough times implies we're doing something good?"

Vee nodded happily.

"So if I happen to live in Ethiopia, where every day is a battle—my situation there is based on whether I'm doing something right or not?"

Vanessa's smile dimmed, and I sighed. "Never mind."

Although I didn't challenge Vanessa about the idea, I wondered how many old wives' tales we Christians trade about life unthinkingly. But then perhaps that's how these notions spread—when we don't have the courage to confront them, they get passed on.

Monday, January 17

I had one of those lovely weekends where not much happened to write about, but it was relaxing and nice. Unfortunately my alarm-clock battery gave up the ghost Saturday night, and I overslept, which meant I missed church. I felt guilty and pleased in almost equal measures. I love our church, but it was wonderful to have that extra couple of hours on Sunday morning to myself. I vacuumed the flat and read the Sunday newspaper. It felt strangely decadent not being in church—sort of naughty and nice.

I got back to work today and hit the ground running. It was a mad day, including a particularly difficult initial home visit to a girl called Hayley, who makes Sissy Spacek in *Carrie* look like Little Bo Peep. Have decided to write in my journal about Hayley—I can't possibly journal here about every child I meet, otherwise this diary is going to feel like a set of case notes, and I'll run out of energy to write it. Suffice it to say that young Hayley is going to be a challenge. She's sixteen and dresses like a stripper with a penchant for white. White shoes, white pedal pushers, white tank top with red diamanté spelling out "1% Angel, 99% Devil" on the bosom. The "1% Angel" bit is probably an exaggeration. "One hundred percent adolescent nightmare" would be more accurate, but then that's a lot of diamanté, and I don't think the tank top is big enough.

Poor girl. She's endured a nightmare upbringing; her Mother spent a decade as a prostitute, with all the terrible scars that would bring—and both she and Hayley's dad have drunk most of any money they've ever earned, either from prostitution or welfare. Finally, rather than have her placed in a foster home, Mrs. Tennant, Hayley's aunt, offered to have her live with her for a while. I had to suspend Hayley's parents' visiting rights over Christmas, as last time she saw them, they'd both ingested way too much alcohol and had a fight. A fight that ended with

Hayley's dad locking her in the bathroom with a knife to her throat, threatening to do her in if her mother didn't break up with some guy called Kevin. It was three hours before the police managed to diffuse the situation. Talk about playing happy families ...

About the only thing that Hayley said today was that with my complexion I couldn't carry off green, my favorite color. Anyway, despite the fact that she obviously loathes me, I hope she managed to enjoy a normal Christmas for once, without all that madness around her. Her aunt seems slightly better adjusted than her parents—*slightly* being the operative word. It's so unfair; some people just don't have a chance in life.

Nothing much else to report. Wrote a letter to Bruno, my brother, who is working on a cruise ship in the Caribbean. I try to send him a few lines every couple of months, although he rarely writes back.

Have now done enough writing for one day. Lord, help me with Hayley. And keep Bruno safe, wherever he is.

Tuesday, January 18

Thank you. Thank you. Thank you. Yes, that would be me lavishing praises on my amazing, generous (and not to mention powerful and loving) Father. God, that is, not my dad, although he is pretty stunning too. You'll never guess what happened to me on the way home! I bumped into

Robert and Nola Marsh, otherwise known as our lovely pastor and his lovely wife.

(Nola, by the way, was wearing a rather stunning blue skirt I saw in the sale at Cats last week, but felt I was a little too rounded to fit into. I must stay off those triple chocolate cookies and perhaps embrace the way of bran muffins in accordance with Mother's advice and move toward a figure more like Keira's.)

After the usual pleasantries, Robert gave me the amazing news. "So, Helen, have you heard about the new staffer? We're getting a worship leader."

Now this could be interesting, especially judging by the grin on Nola's face. "He'll be at church Sunday," she added, with a slight emphasis on he.

"Really?" I tried for nonchalance. "So what's he like?"

"A young fellow. Just graduated from Bible College. Great musician," Robert supplied.

Bingo!

The rest of the conversation basically involved me awkwardly coaxing out details about the man while at the same time trying not to sound like a desperate, single, twenty-seven-year-old. Which of course I am. But oh, was it worth it!

"What's his name?"

"Kristian Vivian Rogers."

Kristian Vivian Rogers. Okay, a little wordy, but not bad. Sort of rolls off the tongue.

"He likes to use all three names." Nola rolled her eyes, and Robert nudged her.

"We were going to introduce him a few weeks ago, but

he felt God calling him to the South of France with some friends, so he's starting this weekend instead."

Yes! He's a worship leader and sensitive to the voice of the missionary God. I'm ecstatic. We're not talking about any old staffer—no! We're not talking some dull-as-dish-water assistant minister or children's worker who thinks that multimedia is a presentation involving a felt board. No, no, no! We are talking about a real in-the-flesh young, enthusiastic, and, most important, male and single worship leader.

I might be in the single Christian girl's fifth heaven. Now all I need to do is quietly assassinate those annoyingly attractive worship band backup singers. I secretly call them the Muppets, because they always take off their shoes and jump around while smiling maniacally at the congregation. I'm sure all that removing of shoes must constitute some sort of health risk ...

I have just looked up the meaning of Kristian and apparently it means "Christian," which, I suppose, is no great revelation. Vivian appears to be a girl's name ... which is worrying ...

Anyway, while I was on the computer checking the meanings of names, I figured that it couldn't do any harm to see if I could find a photo of him. It's not like I was stalking him or anything—in fact, as a member and, indeed, a small-group leader of New Wave Christian Fellowship, I feel that it is my right and duty to know as much as I can about members of our staff leadership team. I googled his Bible college and found a graduation picture of him. He is—wait for it—good-looking! And we are not talking just mildly good-looking, we are talking good-looking in a love-stud, guitar-playing, floppy-blond-hair-and-big-baby-blue-eyes way.

All right, all right, I'm a stalker. But it was worth it.

Just started to daydream about what might be in the future and then remembered the past and felt a tinge of depression ... Okay, Vanessa said I should be brutally honest in my journal.

So ...

I've never had much luck with Christian men. The last Christian guy I dated was at college. Yes, that's the ancient history that was college, about a million years ago. His name was Aaron, and he dumped me because as he was handing out leaflets about the Student Christian Group at the college bar one day, he happened to bump into me. Actually, he didn't bump into me so much as I happened to drunkenly fall off a table and land on his head. He wasn't terribly impressed, and the next day he called me (early in the morning—deliberately, I reckon, because he knew I'd have a thumping hangover) and told me he felt that "we had different agendas." Which basically meant he thought my agenda was to be a drunken Jezebel and his was to be so holy he would forgo death and be whisked to heaven in a flaming chariot or something.

It was stupid of me, I know, but I was a bit intoxicated with the feeling of freedom that slams into a lot of Christian bright young things when they head to college. Hence my overindulgence in tequila that night. It was just one night, and the horrendous experience that I had the next morning cured me for good of getting drunk—but Aaron still dumped me because of it.

The ironic thing is—according to Vanessa, who found out from her cousin's best friend's brother—since finishing college, he's had some sort of existential crisis and has denounced God, quit his job as a bank teller, and now scrawls Friedrich Nietzsche quotes all over his clothes. Vanessa said that her cousin's best friend's brother bumped into Aaron in a park, and he was wandering around mumbling to himself. When asked what was wrong he started to cry and grabbed the guy's shoulders and said something like, "The poor birds, the poor birds … The white bread kills the birds; it expands in their stomachs and chokes them! It's killing them and they don't know it. And it's all because we wanted to make it uniform and all the same. They think that it's food, they're glad to receive it, but it's a lie, a lie that will eventually break them."

And apparently Aaron had the phrase "What have we done?" scrawled across the back of his jacket in office Wite-Out liquid. It sounds like he's completely crazy. And to think that, compared to me at college, he thought of himself as some sort of saint.

I have my mad moments, but not like that. Sometimes I feel like wandering 'round screaming at the world, although I'm not sure what I would say. Knowing me, it would probably be, "Where have all the chocolate cookies gone?" If anything might be the cause for genuine existential panic, a cookie shortage is it.

And so Aaron was the last Christian man I dated. To be honest, my track record with any guy hasn't been too good. I'm hardly what you would call a saint. Everyone sees me as the good girl, but far too often my head has been turned by some guy that I know is completely wrong for me. Sometimes I can't even tell the guys I go out with that I am a Christian because I know they will break up with me, especially if they know that sex is off the cards ... It's just that I've never really been attracted to a Christian guy—not since Aaron anyway, and he obviously didn't think I was good enough for him. So I suppose I gave up.

My friend James, who runs the small group at church with me, is lovely, he really is. Sometimes I think that a romance could work out between the two of us. He's so kind and caring and dependable—he's always ready to help out with the sound desk at church or whatever Robert needs. The problem with James is that I love him in a benignly Christian way, but I don't fancy him. When I think about him kissing me, it grosses me out. I know that's a horrible thing to say about somebody (guilty Helen again). It's not that he's ugly or that there's anything wrong with him at all; he just doesn't "do it" for me.

If I was holier I probably wouldn't care about that. I mean, he's a Christian and lovely, so what more should I want? I know he'd completely look after me. Is it wrong to ask God to help you want to be intimate with someone, or is that weird? Or maybe I'm not supposed to have those feelings before my honeymoon when God will suddenly grant us a lusty love life. I don't know!

But now wonderful worship-leader/boy-band-singer-with-floppy-hair is on the way to Frenton.

I'm excited now and fearful and guilty in almost equal measures ...

God, all I want to do is the right thing, and if that means marrying James I will, because I want to serve you. Please, please, please, give me a husband. I'm so lonely. Is Kristian Vivian Rogers the one? Amen.

Wednesday, January 19

Led our small group tonight with James, which was about prayer. "To be honest, I find prayer rather tough — and sometimes impossible," I ventured, feeling that sudden rush of panic common to Christians who break the ice by being honest in public. "I fall asleep, my mind drifts off to thinking about food, then I end up absentmindedly praying that God would send me a pepperoni pizza. I start off by worshiping the eternal creator and end up treating him like a delivery boy."

I looked around, waiting for the group to pick up stones to rid the planet of the prayerless one. But I was delighted to see that they seemed encouraged by my confession.

The outpouring of honesty began. We talked about how a one-way conversation (which prayer is, much of the time), is hard, and how we have this lingering idea that solitary prayer gets us "more points" with God than prayer that's shared, even though praying together can be easier. Anyway, it was a great, fun evening.

Afterwards I told James about Kristian Vivian Rogers being appointed and for some reason blurted out that I'd seen his photo on the Internet. James didn't look impressed about my web surfing or excited about us getting a new worship leader.

It's been a tough day. I went to see Hayley, and the sum total of our little chat was that she told me to go away immediately by repeatedly yelling two words (thirty-five times), neither of which I would put in my journal.

Called Dad to offload a bit, but his cell phone wasn't on; he was probably in a council committee meeting. I shed a couple of tears and obviously still looked upset when I got back to the office.

Laura, who so far is the only person there who has made a serious effort to befriend me, gave me some advice. "Hang in there. You never can tell with these kids. You might think that someone's as hard as old boots on the surface, but they could be as gooey as a chocolate brownie underneath."

"Hmm … I wish that was the case with Hayley. So far all she's shown me is boot leather—the old nasty kind that's been tromping through bogs for years until you can't even bend it anymore."

"Well, even if that's the case, my dear, so what? If she's boot leather, she's boot leather."

I must have looked unconvinced. She clarified.

"Helen, it doesn't matter if you get results or not; the point is that you do what you do because, well, it's the right thing to do. It doesn't matter whether it works or not."

I thought about that, yet Jesus did loads of good things

and they always seemed to get a result. I seem to get abuse or disinterest. Then I thought some more and realized that most of the good things that Jesus did actually got him rejected and into hot water and ultimately nailed to a cross.

Lord, please help me have more effect at work; I feel like I'm banging my head against a brick wall.

However, Laura does believe in being firm with Hayley. Laura met Hayley when she came to the office demanding money. Apparently Hayley gave her a mouthful because she had to wait in reception for twenty minutes because appointments were running late. Hayley started screaming, and Laura held up her hand.

"Shout at this, sweetie, 'cause that's the only thing that's going to respond. Yelling won't get you anywhere here."

And at that, Hayley sat down and shut up, though the fixed scowl on her face didn't budge for twenty minutes.

Sometimes I wish I could have Laura's no-nonsense no-fear confidence, yet mingled with kindness too. Tonight after house group I read Genesis 9, which is where Noah spent a little too long at the grape trough and ended up totally stoned (felt a little relieved about my old college lapse). Whereupon his son Ham (who was such a nasty piece of work that pork was named after him) made a laughingstock of his dad. Whereas the other two sons, Shem and Japheth, covered their father's nakedness and preserved his dignity. Had to banish unhelpful fantasy of George Clooney playing legless Noah in a tent and my coming svelte-like to his rescue ...

(Am I the only Christian who is actually so frustrated

that she's even found reading a passage in the Bible excit-ing? Robert's sermon on the Song of Solomon last year was a delight in some rather unhelpful ways …)

Once I'd managed to send that delicious notion pack-ing, I couldn't help thinking that some Christians are like Ham—they seem to get a real thrill out of seeing others fail and struggle. Thought about Mr. and Mrs. Hemming again; decided that I preferred to think about Mr. Clooney in a tent.

Tired again. Have prayed for dreams that don't feature George in an Old Testament *Waterworld*, with Kevin Cost-ner as Ham. But am not sure I want that prayer answered. Didn't say amen. It must have been the thought of George and Kevin and *Waterworld*, but I suddenly remembered my dad taking me fishing at the end of the pier when I was about five. My fishing line got totally entangled around the reel, and after a few seconds of trying to sort it, I handed it to Dad, who spent the next fifteen minutes carefully and patiently unpicking the knots.

Lord, sometimes I feel overwhelmed and lost inside my own head. There are so many thoughts, motives, fears, and hopes, all messed up in a bunch like a tangled fishing line. Help me not so much to untangle the sorry mess, but to hand it over to you. Amen.

This idea of journal honesty is being tested to the limit. I had the strangest dream last night—and when I say strange, I mean completely and utterly weird. Even Sigmund Freud would edge slowly and carefully away from me. I need to be instantly committed to an asylum, covered from head to foot in holy oil produced in Israel, prayed over by nuns for forty days and forty nights, and exorcised with a ceremony involving garlic. The dream was so sick I can't even remember it without feeling like I need the internal equivalent of a 90-degree wash. Gross. I won't repeat the sordid details, because if anyone ever found this diary I would die of shame. But call me Helen "so perverse there aren't even names for the things she did in her dreams last night" Sloane. And the worst thing was I woke up and wanted to nod off immediately so that I could get back into the dream. There, I've said it: I am a pervert and should be locked up for the sake of other people's safety.

Katy, one of the Riverdancing backup singers at church and a member of our small group, was talking only last night about how sometimes she wakes up praying. Praying! A whole tent of circus performers couldn't recreate what I woke up dreaming, even if you included the menagerie. God, please cleanse my mind so this doesn't happen again. Why can't I be like Julie Andrews or Mother Teresa or Katy? I bet they've never had this problem ...

Blah kind of workday mostly involving admin catch-ups with nothing of note to report. Before sleeping, I showered, prayed for a looooooooooooong time (being a pervert, I need all the help I can get), read not only my daily section of the Bible, but also the one I didn't read yesterday, and—because you never know—read tomorrow's as well. I then sang along, very badly (sorry, God) with a new worship CD, which I kept playing quietly all night. Slept fitfully but managed to avoid any more perverse dreams. Thank God for the power of prayer.

Part of my marathon Bible-reading stint was the Sodom and Gomorrah incident (Gen. 19), which describes the mad, desperate need for sex in that city and the brutality and perversity of the place. I was strangely comforted by the vile story because I realized that I live in a sick world that's crawling with nasty ideas and images: no wonder my mind sometimes trips a breaker and dreams sicko stuff like I did the other night. On reflection, perhaps I'm not such a terrible sinner after all. I'd assumed that journaling was supposed to make me feel bad about myself, what with all that introspection, but am now finding out that sometimes it makes me feel better. I wondered whether that happened to that crusty Simeon Stylites, the pole sitter.

Lord, help me to live for you. The world's sometimes a horrid place and it rubs off. Amen.

It being Sunday, as usual I attended the service at New Wave. But this was no ordinary day! It was an eventful, even epic, morning, and not just because of the arrival of man of God Kristian. (Blessed is he who comes in the name of the Lord!) K. V. Rogers, or K.V., as I called him during the entirely imaginary conversations that I had with him in my head today, is even better looking than his Google photo portrays, all fresh and blond and tanned from his outreach in the South of France. I have no idea what kind of mission he was on, but it sounded like he was doing a lot of open-air ministry, as he mentioned being on the beach a lot. What a bold, courageous, tanned, godly, tanned, spiritually sensitive, tanned young man he is!

He does have one teeny-weeny imperfection. After leading worship (wonderfully, I must say), he handed the service back to Robert, who was our preacher for the morning. But I noticed that when Kristian sat down (on the pew in front of mine—tell me that's not God!), he put his guitar back in its stand and then sat back and didn't seem to pay any attention to what Robert said at all. He didn't open a Bible (don't think he even had one). He did start scribbling something—at first I thought that maybe he was making notes about the sermon and was concentrating hard, but then I leaned over to take a closer look and saw that he was actually writing a poem, or something like that. When he began writing guitar chords over the words, I realized he was writing a new worship song during dear lovely Robert's sermon, which I thought was a bit off.

I tried to tell myself that Kristian is in fact a tanned King David prophetic-psalmist type whose creative muse is the preaching of the Scriptures, but if I'm honest I fear that he might be a little bit too interested in his own stuff and not terribly attentive to any teaching. But this is but a mere foible, a trifling issue compared to his immense anointing as a leader ... and his perfect teeth. And did I mention his tan?

Anyway, his lack of attention was certainly his loss, because Robert's sermon was nothing short of stunning, fabulous, and wonderful. In fact, it usually is. Robert is an inspiration: he's down to earth, vulnerable, and funny but always manages to nudge us to think about our faith. One or two members of our little congregation aren't so keen on him, especially Mr. and Mrs. Hemming.

Realized when I saw them both this morning that I hadn't nursed any thoughts about murdering her lately, which might be an answer to prayer—or maybe simply because my mind has been too preoccupied with the coming of K.V. Mr. Hemming always wears the same suit and the same frown on Sundays, as if he believes that God wants us all to assume an expression suggesting that we are suffering from severe constipation and are in need of much bran. Perhaps I should print out Mum's Caribbean Explosion Diet for him.

And not only is Mrs. Hemming such a gifted "sharer," but she seems to love catching people doing something wrong. Actually, I need to put that differently. What Mrs.

Hemming actually loves doing is catching people doing things that she doesn't like, which includes singing new worship songs, not using a version of the Bible that was translated at least three hundred years or so ago, or—the crime that is tantamount to blasphemy and deserves a burning—reorganizing the chairs in what she calls "the sanctuary."

Mr. and Mrs. Hemming are a walking demonstration that there is a just God out there because they definitely deserve each other. They sat through Robert's sermon on "Running the Race" with faces so long you'd have thought he'd announced that he was going to preach while naked. It was a fabulous message. Robert pointed out that Paul the Apostle was into sports, what with all those analogies about running and chariot racing, wrestling and boxing. Mrs. Hemming definitely didn't approve and shot one of those sneery looks at her husband when Robert mentioned wrestling, which she probably lists as a carnal pursuit. I had an unholy and rather nauseating thought about Mr. and Mrs. Hemming engaging in wrestling, which I swiftly banished.

Robert spoke powerfully and honestly, and I realized why our home group has felt so comfortable with airing their struggles about prayer:

"The Christian life calls for faithfulness and discipline," said Robert, without a hint of rant. "Sometimes I just don't feel like 'doing' faith. In fact, if I followed my feelings, I'd be in a right mess. There are seasons when we feel nothing, but disciplined choices can sustain us through those desert experiences."

I was instantly challenged, which I sometimes think is Christian code for "feeling bad." My lack of good discipline is an issue, and my chocolate-cookie problem obviously needs a firm hand, there being no support groups like Alcoholics Anonymous: "Hi, I'm Helen, and I'm addicted to chocolate muffins, cookies, and all things made of chocolate ..."

So ...

I have decided to literally run the race. Yes, I, Helen Sloane, am going to run a marathon this year. Training begins tomorrow. I shall decide on a good cause, pester my friends for sponsorship, raise some cash, lose some pounds in fat, and become a woman in control of her life.

There were a couple of other happenings in the service. I went forward for prayer in response to Robert's sermon, to make firm my determination to become a marathoner. But then my mind wandered during the prayer. James came out to the front and stood with me while I was being prayed for, which was lovely, but I couldn't help thinking about a bronzed, blond psalmist of the Lord during the praying. He was strumming his guitar quietly during the prayer, providing a sort of divine backing music, and everyone started singing a worship song that talked about "kissing the Lord with our praises." Unfortunately, I found myself singing the song while thinking about kissing luscious Kristian.

And then, to make it worse, when the prayer was over James swept me into one of those "Oh, I love you in the Lord, most precious sister" hugs, which lasted two or three seconds longer than it probably needed to, and I felt even more guilty about my longings for closer fellowship with our new worship leader.

After the service, I went over to Mum and Dad's for one of Mum's epic Sunday lunches: roast beef, Yorkshire pudding, roasted potatoes. I didn't mention my niggling desire to sweep our new worship leader off his feet, but while Mum was putting the finishing touches to her culinary masterpiece in the kitchen, I told Dad about the hilarious happenings when it came to communion.

"Mrs. Hemming is in charge of preparing the bread and wine and she guards that responsibility like a Rottweiler on crack, Dad."

Dad nodded and I knew he understood. He's dealt with plenty of control freaks in his life.

"She threatened to leave the church last year when Robert suggested that a rotation list be created so that others could share the privilege. She said that this was her God-given ministry in the fellowship and nobody was going to take it away from her. After all, she said, women should not preach."

"New Wave doesn't buy that anti-women stuff, does it?" said Dad, suddenly a little alarmed.

"No, Dad. It's not what our church believes, just Mr. and Mrs. Hemming, because they think that females are likely to lead the brethren astray just as Eve did with her shapely hips and good-looking apple. So, Mrs. H argues that preparing communion is her way of serving the Lord."

Dad sighed. "From what you've told me about Mrs. Hemming, Helen, it sounds like she'd do better serving the Lord with a lengthy vow of silence." I smiled.

"Anyway, Dad, apparently Mrs. Hemming hadn't realized that all the wine had been used last week. She believes that Sunday shopping is going to earn wayward Sabbath breakers an eternal grilling on God's hellish barbecue, so she refused to allow anyone to go to the shops to get some more. The only thing available was some raspberry Jell-O left over from the Prime Timers Christmas party, so Mrs. Hemming announced that the Lord had truly provided, diluted the Jell-O sufficiently (or so she thought), poured the purple concoction into those little cups, and placed the trays of holy Jell-O under the white napkins on the communion table.

"Sadly (or perhaps providentially) Robert's sermon was quite long; the prayer time after it took longer than usual because so many people responded, and so, by the time we got to taking communion, it had set solid. It's tough trying to reverently scoop up such a holy emblem with one's little finger. One lad at the back who was obviously too young to partake loudly asked where the whipped cream was, seeing as we were having Jell-O. But it was a wonderful moment, mainly because Mrs. Hemming looked fit to bust."

Dad laughed out loud, and I suddenly realized that one of my favorite sounds is that of my dad laughing. Mum came in with a heaving tray of roast potatoes, and Dad insisted that I recount the whole saga again for her. And he laughed all over again the second time. I do love him so.

There was a sad postscript though: Mr. Hemming got into a row with Robert right after the service. It was Robert's fault, said Mr. Hemming, that his wife had been so mortally embarrassed by the setting Jell-O. His sermons should be shorter and what was the need for times of prayer anyway? Robert tried to respond, but in the end I think he gave up. Sometimes religious people lose the capacity to listen.

Anyway, I am now a marathon runner in training, an athlete on their way to sporting glory, like Eric Liddell of *Chariots of Fire* fame. Step aside, Keira, here I come ...

Monday, January 24

What a morning! I felt a little discouraged that oxygen seems so very elusive after just half a mile of running, but even Eric Liddell started somewhere. I told Laura at work about my marathon decision. She's a runner, so she gave me some great advice.

"Just decide, Helen. Decide that, from now on, there's no ifs, buts, or excuses. No discussion allowed in your head. Just run. Every day."

I got to my desk to be greeted by a work avalanche. It seems like every childcare case in Frenton landed on my desk over the weekend.

Then I went over to Hayley's aunt and uncle's this afternoon. Hayley was out shopping so I had to sit and wait for her. It was difficult to chat to Hayley's aunt, as she talks endlessly and doesn't think listening is part of a conversation. Not only that, but she'd been drinking; the sour smell of whisky made my stomach turn.

Hayley's aunt glared at me as she chugged on what was, judging by the overflowing ashtray on the coffee table, her ten millionth cigarette that afternoon. "You social workers, you're always sticking your nose in, aren't yer? You know better than everyone else, don't yer, Miss stuck-up duffel-coat lady?"

She paused to cough and enjoy the fruits of her lifelong investment in the Marlboro tobacco company. "We don't need your help, you hear? We're all right. Hayley's high-spirited, that's all. All kids are like that. I used to be like Hayley, and I turned out okay."

Thought about that statement and put together a reply in my head but decided not to share it . . .

"Mrs. Tennant," I tried to reply politely, "not all teenagers tie flaming pieces of garbage onto the tail of a dog and push the poor creature through their neighbor's windows whilst screaming, 'Release the hounds!'" I had to pause again to allow Mrs. Tennant space for a good minute's rasping coughing, as well as a couple more puffs. "I know Hayley has had a difficult home life, and I am trying to ensure there's a more stable environment for her so she can overcome these behavioral problems."

With that, Hayley stomped through the door, an expression of complete thunder on her face, took one look at me, and shared a warm greeting.

"Yo, it's the stuck-up witch from the council."

"Excuse me," I replied, trying to reinstate my authority and show that I'm not scared of these two maniac women —and praying of course in my head that God would grant me the power of some *über* angel so I could turn them both into pillars of salt. But apparently I couldn't summon up an intimidating enough pose because Hayley let rip and it wasn't pretty. I'd write it down in here, but frankly the presence of all those profanities might turn these pages blue. The long and the short of it was that by denying Hayley Christmas with her family, I had also denied her a new Game Boy, an MP3 player, a smart phone, Britney Spears' new perfume, and goodness knows what other clothes and gadgets. Apparently her mum and dad like to make up for their complete lack of parental care and responsibility by lavishing her with things (which they probably can't afford and must go on their credit cards). Now Hayley can't possibly show her face in public because her cell phone is a whole six months old and her MP3 player only holds eight hundred songs and she needs to download the whole of P. Diddy's back catalogue from a friend's iPod.

I've seriously considered giving up social work for good today ...

Lord, the worst thing was this: I was actually frightened of her. I was terrified of a sixteen-year-old kid. As a Christian, I know I'm supposed to be all confident in you and have faith that you will protect me in that kind of situation. But to be honest, I couldn't get out of there fast enough. Her aunt was probably too drunk to hit me that hard, but Hayley—she looked like once she'd started she'd never stop.

That poor, strange frightening little girl ...

When I'm in a church service it all seems so easy to have faith in you. When I'm praying, I'm full of all these fantasies about being some sort of Christian Buffy the

Vampire Slayer, who, when confronted with situations like that, ends up rebuking the hatred in Jesus' name, saying something incredibly meaningful and profound, and leading the whole room to Christ. It always seems to work in the Bible; why doesn't it ever seem to work today?

As I left, I wondered what kind of person Hayley might have been if she'd been brought up with some basics like love and security. How different would she have been if her parents had talked to her? All she ever got from her home life were lessons in drinking and violence.

And all that musing about the power of love and relationships got me thinking about my confession the other day about sex, and I've realized it's not just sex that I want. Well, obviously, yes, I definitely want the sex. But it's more about the intimacy that surrounds sex. You know, those long mornings snuggled up in bed, having pillow fights and feeding each other strawberries. Okay! I've seen far too many movies, but something vaguely along those lines would be great. I mean, it's hard to be alone and not have that kind of intimacy with anyone. I think that's what humans were made for. After all, Adam was supposed to have had a perfect relationship with God, yet he still wanted the intimacy with Eve that companionship brings. Snuggling up and teasing each other with what I'm sure will be hilariously witty banter; having someone hug you and hug you without it becoming awkward and a bit embarrassing. Plus, they'd be someone to make you hot tea in the mornings and perhaps even bring you a couple of chocolate cookies. Sounds like heaven to me ...

God, please bless and guide and preserve Kristian.

May he settle into our church easily and develop one or two good, close, loving friendships very quickly. Or maybe just one of those good, close, and loving friendships would be sufficient. Amen.

Wonder if there was a strawberry patch in Eden. Or music.

Tuesday, January 25

Didn't manage to run at all today ... must get Laura to give me her little speech again. And must sort out which charity I am going to run for ...

Horrific news! My fifty-six-year-old mother has pierced her nose. Yes, my fifty-six-year-old, Chanel No. 5 – wearing mother went to the tattoo and piercing parlor and got her nose punctured.

"He was a lovely man, a real artist, darling, who rejoices in the name of Killer," Mum said when I called her. "And he's a living billboard for the creativity of tattooing. The ink colors of the snake strangling a kitten on his forearm were amazing. I just love my piercing."

Apparently the crystal nose-stud "projects" her nasal ley line so it can "interact" with her moon-star chakra, which (according to her best friend Babs) will make sure that nothing bad ever happens to her again, ever, period. You also have to send an offering to some guru called Bshach Yabba, who lives in a permanent state of serenity in India. Babs has returned from her own personal pilgrimage to India, and apparently it was very relaxing, apart from (according to her) "those nasty little beggar children putting their grubby fingers over my prayer shawl." God forbid that the poor of the earth might hijack Babs' odd spirituality ...

How come that I did something so simple as inviting Jesus into my life when I was ten, when my mother (who packed me off to Sunday school with the advice that it would do me good) has gotten into all this bizarre stuff?

The worst thing about my mother's nose-piercing is that it won't actually look too bad. She may be fifty-six, but I strongly suspect she is more attractive than me. She certainly dresses better. Last week she was wearing skinny jeans. Yes, I said my mother wears skinny jeans! I can't even pull off skinny jeans. Or more precisely, I can't even pull on skinny jeans. Not past my knees anyway.

My parents live in a quaint little village, just outside of Frenton, which has a post office that only opens once a month. The village is very picturesque—horribly boring but pretty in a Beatrix Potterish kind of way. Mum and Dad live in a cottage designed for hobbits—specifically hobbits with a penchant for hanging crystals and wind chimes from every available outdoor surface. When the wind blows, it sounds like an explosion in a glass factory.

Speaking of chimes, my parents both attend the local village church. Dad seems to get it, and he's been a real support to the local vicar, lending a hand with the accounts when the church's somewhat elderly church treasurer unfortunately and suddenly disappeared with a woman thirty years his junior, a hairdresser called Tracey.

Dad and I have had some great chats about God; he knows the Bible really well. He's not loud about faith though, and he does seem to have a bit of a blind spot when it comes to my mum, because she doesn't seem to get Christianity at all. She believes in God, but sometimes she gives me the impression that her belief is in whatever god of the week is in vogue. She thinks that all spirituality is fine, as long as it vaguely involves being nice to each other . . . and incense. She's not sure what a religion should contain, but if it doesn't involve setting fire to things that smell nice and funny mumbling, then she's not interested.

I wish Dad would talk to her about it more and help put her on the straight and narrow, but he doesn't. I think that the poor man is hopelessly besotted with her and believes that she'll sort it all out in her own way and time. All of which means that when Mum mentioned her new crystal nasal appendage on the phone this morning, I decided to pop 'round for a viewing tonight and perhaps have a chat about her pick-'n'-mix spirituality.

I let myself in, banged my head on the hobbit door frame, and called, "Mum? Dad? Are you around?"

"Daaaarling, is that you?" Mum's voice echoed down the hallway. "Come up here. I'm in the bath, so plop yourself down and we'll have a nice chat."

When I was younger most of the quality time between my mum and me was spent in the bathroom, with me perched on the closed toilet lid whilst my mother luxuriated in the bath, sandalwood aromatherapy candle flickering, gripping a glass of red wine with her perfectly manicured fingernails. "Look, daaarling, look, look what mummy Kitty's done! I've gone and pierced my nose. How naughty am I!"

My mother keeps trying to get me to call her Kitty like all her friends do. She says the word "Mother" makes her feel old. I love her desperately, but want her to stay in her current role as my mum and not turn me into another one of her friends in the "ladies that lunch" set ...

"Darling, you look tired. I do hope you've not been overdoing it. You could do with some fun! Tell you what, I'll take you shopping next weekend ..."

And then she went on about how Babs was a brand new person as a result of her Indian epiphany and that she's going to London next week for a colonic irrigation, because apparently all that purging helps you focus ... We nattered back and forth happily because, despite my mum being so intergalactic, she always seems to realize in time that she's been rambling on, and makes room for me to chat—which is nice, but also creates a problem, which I'll try to explain in a moment ...

Then suddenly and without warning, my mother gets out the bath, with, as-per-usual, absolutely no modesty whatsoever. I get horribly embarrassed every time she strides around naked, which is frequently, often when she's doing the housework. She tried to get my father to join a naturist group once; thank God, he refused, and she said there was no point going without him. She hates doing things without my dad. Though I like to think my desperate prayers had something to do with it.

Anyway, she's sitting on the edge of the bath wrapped

in a towel (another answered prayer) looking a little more closely at me.

"Darling, are you okay? You look tired."

"Oh. Um … I'm fine Mum—just lots to do at work—and church has been … well, quite demanding lately."

I desperately wanted to tell her about the three people who are making me lose sleep at the moment. I could mention nightmare Hayley, who sometimes appears in dreams that feature teenagers armed with chainsaws. Or Mr. and Mrs. Hemming, who use the Bible like a chainsaw. I'm not sure which of these oh-so-difficult people upsets me more.

But here's the problem: with Mum somewhat up in the air about her faith (sometimes she's not so much as high as a kite as cruising at 36,000 feet like a jumbo jet) I feel reluctant to tell her about my struggles. I worry that she'll think that my faith in Jesus doesn't work (thus nudging her towards ever weirder spiritual safaris) or that the church is full of hypocrites (once again nudging her towards ever weirder spiritual safaris).

And so when she asks me how I'm doing, I lie. "But I'm fine. Just a little tired. The job's really pulling at me right now."

She looks a bit suspicious, but I don't say anything. I end up being dishonest with my own mother, creating obvious distance between us, at least from my side. I think she senses that I'm not letting her into my struggles, which worries me, because I'd hate to hurt her. I do so love her. (Even though her willowy body—even when naked—makes me envious. If my body was a tree, it wouldn't be a willow—it's more like an oak. And "oaky" isn't a good description for anything except Chardonnay.)

"Well, if you say so, dear." Mum bustled off to dry her hair, and since I hate trying to continue a chat with a 900-watt turbo dryer on at full blast, I took the opportunity to wander off to find my dad. Mum had said he's on one of his little campaigns.

"He's at it again, darling. You know how upset he got over the" (and here she mouthed the words silently, as if mentioning the unmentionable) "'battle of the beach huts' affair ... Well, now he's fighting another just war ..."

The battle of the beach huts is a campaign that we don't like to talk about much in our house. My father is a retired bank manager, but, as I said, he also works part time for the local government as a councilor. A couple of years ago, there was a big scandal involving a proposal to build new beach huts. They were going to be located down a stretch of beach that was completely unsuitable: there were no toilets, no proper parking and apparently, in the winter, the tide could be so severe that it might even wash them away. There was one councilor whose family business was a building company, and he wanted to give his brother permission to build on this stretch of beach so they could sell the huts off at an extortionate price to unsuspecting citizens.

My father found out about the nasty little scheme and went mad. He tried to generate a community-wide pro-test against the blatant corruption but ended up not only losing the debate (the council flexed its muscles and Dad suspects some under-the-counter political deals), but he almost had to give up his seat on the council because of it.

Dad's such a mild-mannered man, and I don't think he's sore for himself because he lost—it's that he hates it when the fat cats win. He says that he spent a lifetime as a banker in the city watching the big boys throw their weight around and lobbing people's lives onto the scrapheap for the sake of a fast buck, and so now when he sees that kind of behavior in our community, he'll half-kill himself to fight it.

I wandered into his study and found him with his nose in a law book, obviously preparing for his next battle. It's amazing how little actions can make someone so completely lovable. As I walked in, Dad put his book down and closed it without putting a bookmark in it and stood up to give me a hug. It's a genuine gesture that makes me feel like I'm the exclusive focus of his attention. I feel a bit guilty now as I look back on the moment, because I didn't even ask him about his new battle, but launched almost immediately into my woes about the Hemmings and Hayley.

He smiled and nodded and I'm sure that at one point he wiped away a tear. I wasn't sure whether that was for Hayley, because she's been so messed up, or for me, because he can see that I'm stretched to the limit.

"I do worry about you darling," he said, "because in so many ways, you're so much like me. Once I get my teeth into something, I won't let go, and then I get anxious and end up exhausted. I do worry that I've passed on some of my genetic intensity to you. I hate to see that lovely brow of yours looking so furrowed."

Then he said, "It's tough, Helen, when you're investing in the invisible. And that's what you do when you pour yourself into other people's lives: there's no gauge that says that they're listening, that they care what you think, that anything you're doing is helpful. You don't win every battle, and sometimes you don't win any. But people are worth fighting for. So while I don't want you to wear yourself out, do keep going with Hayley. Sometimes icebergs take almost forever to thaw. And don't fret about the Hemmings, because a dose of religion is no guarantee that irritating and stupid people will be less irritating and stupid."

He didn't really tell me anything I don't know, but as a result of my chat with Dad, I did decide (a) not to abandon social work to embrace a new career as a fuller-figure supermodel and (b) not to kill anyone with an "H" in their name, like Hemming or Hayley.

Wednesday, January 26

Can only write one line today and it's urgent and desperate. Please, please, please, God, I'll do anything—but let Hayley be found safely. Please. Amen. Please.

Thursday, January 27

More of the same. She's still missing. The police are involved now. Please. Please.

Friday, January 28

Okay, some explanations. Wednesday I got a phone call from Hayley's hideous aunt telling me that Hayley hadn't come home. "She's a real handful, that one. A tear-away, just like me when I was a kid, I suppose."

I tried to imagine Mrs. Tennant as a young person but can only imagine that she was born in her mid-fifties with a cigarette in her mouth, which must have been alarming for the midwife.

Mrs. Tennant continued, "Apparently, she went out to see some friends—they tend to hang around by the pier and eat fish and chips—but she didn't come back at the end of the evening. She's not answering her cell phone, none of her friends that the police have contacted so far have any idea where she is—or if they do, they're not saying—and the coppers are drawing a blank."

Auntie paused, and I felt her disgust through the phone line. Clearly she'd decided Hayley was missing because I've been negligent in some way and haven't provided Hayley with the support that she needs.

I was horrified. "I–I don't know what to say. I'm so sorry."

She grunted. "Well, seeing as how we need to be out looking, I don't have time to chat. I just figured you should know."

Again the implication that I should or could do something. Miserable, I said my good-byes.

"Oh, God. What have I done?" I'm so good at guilt, I immediately decided it was my fault — that I haven't done everything right and that I might have allowed Hayley's abusive tirades to lessen my professional care for her. I even went through her case notes three times to check on the frequencies of my home visits and make sure that I kept all the appointments that I made with her. And I had. But I still feel that somehow I might be to blame. Did I leave their house too early the other day because I was scared? If I'd stayed a little longer, might there have been a conversation that could have prevented Hayley from going missing?

Please, God, let her be found. The police are talking about putting posters around the town with her photograph. Please, please, God.

Tonight James and Vanessa came out to walk around the town with me, in the vain hope that we might find her hanging out with one of the gaggle of kids who horse around in the streets. James was great and was quite bold. I felt nervous about approaching one group of older kids, who looked stoned and dodgy, to ask if they knew Hayley, so James marched right up to them and managed a chat with no problem. They didn't know her, but I thought that it was nice of James to put himself out like that.

And then Vanessa was lovely too. She was praying out

loud, quietly but continuously, as we walked around the town. I'd never have the nerve to do something like that, and yet it was wonderfully comforting to hear her whispering her prayers while we walked. It kept reminding me that we are not on our own in times like this. Thank God for God—and thank God for friends.

Please, God, may Hayley be found. Keep her safe and I'll do everything I can to help her, if you'll give me wisdom. Amen.

Saturday, January 29

Hayley is a selfish, obnoxious little cow, and I don't like her one bit. She showed up at her house last night and seemed completely unmoved by all the fuss. Apparently, she started chatting to an older lad at the pier last Tuesday night—and they stayed chatting after all of her other friends had gone home. He lives in a trailer on one of the residential sites here, and so when he invited her back for the night, she agreed and basically hung out with him doing Lord knows what for the last three days and only came home last night because she'd run out of money and he was broke.

I went to see her this afternoon, and she was horrible, refused to tell me what she and her boyfriend had been up to and, in fact, barely spoke to me at all. She answered every question I asked her with the same response.

"Why did you go with him?"

"I'm bored."

"Didn't you think that everyone would be worried about you?"

"I'm bored."

"Did he hurt you?"

"Everything's boring."

"What can I do to help you, Hayley?"

"Why not shut up for a start? You're soooo boring."

For thirty minutes Hayley said the same thing over and over again, and then it hit me.

She's bored.

When I got back to the office, I had a little chat with Laura about it.

"Something needs to be done for all these kids who hang out at the pier," she said. "The streets at night are dangerous. Something needs to be done to take them off the streets and give them some safe, alternative things to do. Someone needs to do something. That might not solve all of the problems of someone like Hayley, but it would be a start. It might stop some other kids ending up with bigger issues than they have already."

She's right.

Sunday, January 30

I read Exodus 29 this morning, which is about Aaron being chosen and anointed as a priest. I wondered what it would be like to be picked out by God to do something special ...

Church was good this morning. Mrs. Hemming was complaining again (loudly, so almost everyone could hear) over the after-service cup of tea. "I feel deeply troubled in my spirit, I can tell you," she said to nobody in particular. "The sermon just wasn't enough today. I didn't get a thing out of it. It was shallow, superficial waffle. No depth." She paused and then threw in the kicker. "I tell you, we're not being fed in this church."

Ouch. It's so difficult to defend yourself against that one. But someone did. Nola, our ever kind wife to Robert, strode over to Mrs. H. She took Mrs. Hemming's empty teacup with a little more force than was necessary, which was marvelous, and then spoke up, her eyes flashing.

"I wonder if you really managed to catch everything Robert was saying, Mrs. Hemming, or to appreciate the amount of study and preparation that went into that sermon that you so despised. You did appear to be whispering to your husband through most of it, so perhaps you didn't hear that much?"

And with that, Nola swept away, leaving Mrs. Hemming speechless, which is a miracle on a par with Lazarus coming out of his tomb. I love Nola.

I wandered up to Kristian, almost shoved one of the Barbie-doll worship singers out of the way, and introduced myself.

"Nice to meet you, Hel," he said.

I smiled. "It's *Helen*."

He ignored me. "It's so great to be here in the church.

Really wonderful place, Hel. Great vibe, don't you think?" This was followed by a three-minute monologue about how he's enjoying the church and how this week he managed to write three new songs. He called me Hel throughout it.

No one calls me Hel. I hate being called Hel. I don't want people to think of me and subliminally connect my personality with eternal conscious torment, which is how Mrs. Hemming describes that place. I'm sure I'll eventually be able to teach Kristian to call me something else. Like *honey*.

Darling would be fine.

I thought again about my chat with Laura and the pier kids.

Prayed once more that someone would do something about them.

Monday, January 31

Prayed again that someone would do something for these kids.

Wednesday, February 2

Suggested to James that we spend some time at the small group praying that someone would do something for the kids. He agreed that we should and so we did. During the prayer, Katy said she had a picture of a pier that had been devastated by a storm and half of it had been swept away. Some of the group thought that this meant that the kids had been so damaged by the storms of life. I quietly thought that this was mad because (a) that's obvious and (b) Frenton does have a pier that has been devastated by a storm and half of it has been swept away. Sometimes my fellow Christians make me wonder … has all the maniacal jigging done by Katy and the worship backing girlies done something to their brains?

Afterward, James walked me home, and we had a conversation that turned into something rather terrifying.

"What do you think of Katy, James?" I asked, probing a little to find out what he thought about her "revelations."

"Oh, she's nice enough, and very pretty, but she seems a little too given to hearing things from God. Funny, isn't it, Helen, that some people seem to go overboard with their spirituality, but it's very difficult to challenge them about it. I could never be with someone like that."

Be with? What did he mean?

"You mean … marry someone like Katy, James?"

"Exactly, Helen. I would quite like to be married, you know. But I want someone who is fun, certainly full of life, but solid and dependable too. Someone that I can really talk things through with, who cares deeply, but doesn't go over the top." And then James proceeded to tell me the further details of what he's looking for in a wife, and after he gave me the briefest of hugs goodnight, I found myself sitting in my flat, wrestling with a rather horren-

dous question: Could it be that the ideal person for him
… is *me*?

Thursday, February 3

Spent restless night worrying about possible romantic over-
tures from James and then, over breakfast, decided that I
have other things to be concerned about. Have decided that
perhaps I should do something about these kids.

I can't.

I'm too busy.

I'm already involved in too much.

I scarcely have any time for myself as it is. I got together
with Vanessa tonight, with a view of talking it all out. It
was a great evening. After the dreadful few days of worry
about Hayley going missing, it was good to be a bit giggly
and silly. That's what is great about Vanessa — she may be
odd but she's a laugh.

We also had a good pray as well and spent some time
thanking God for Hayley being safe — am now able to pray
that and mean it.

We had a deep chat about prayer too.

Vanessa was enthusing: "I am finding more and more
that I love to pray, Helen. It's a bit like a hunger or an
addiction. When I walk along the boardwalk, and just talk
to Jesus, I feel such an amazing sense of peace — it's difficult to describe. But I feel excited about it, like going on
a date."

My heart sank.

"I envy you, Vee. I tend to think about prayer as a chore, something that good Christians are supposed to do. And I'm sure I can cope with the idea that prayer is exciting, like dating — in fact, I get a bit weary of those worship songs where I'm always having to tell Jesus that I love him, in a sort of romantic way, whereas I do love him, but not like that, obviously. And sometimes I just don't feel anything."

Vanessa was undeterred. "But isn't that where faith comes in, Helen? We're called to walk each day with God, whatever we feel like. But there's still something really exciting about knowing that God hears us and answers too."

"Mmm. I'm not so sure, Vee. I've decided that unanswered prayer isn't the problem — it's answered prayer that's the real challenge. With children dying every day in Africa, isn't any request from us relatively rich people in the West a bit frivolous and low on God's list of priorities? Why should God bother with any of it? I struggle sometimes with the thought that it's perhaps even mildly obscene that we talk to him about our money, coughs and colds, choice of car, who we'll marry, and a thousand and one other comparative trivialities."

Vee smiled. "I get that, Helen. And yet God is interested, isn't he?"

As Vee and I chatted on, I felt selfish because once again I'd brought the conversation right back down to me. I'm ashamed to admit it, but it niggles me a bit to realize that God did apparently answer our prayers about finding

Hayley, but all my fervent intercessions about my love life have taken me nowhere.

Then we got talking about the problem of bored kids in Frenton and Vanessa grabbed my hand. "We need to pray about it, right now, Helen. It's an urgent matter. God loves these kids. Someone needs to do something for these kids."

And so we prayed. But I already knew. I've got to do something for these kids.

Sunday, February 6

Nice weekend. Had another seven-minute chat with Kristian after the service yesterday morning, when he asked me repeatedly how I felt he was doing as the church's new worship leader.

"It's a difficult gig, Hel," he said. "Creativity needs context, and I'm still settling in, and sometimes I feel a bit awkward, a bit closed in. Besides, Robert is insisting that the sung-worship part of the service should only last thirty minutes, which I feel could stifle things a bit. I need that amount of time to get into the flow, you know what I mean, Hel?"

I felt a bit uncomfortable with him criticizing Robert like that. Kristian's welcome to his opinions, but I was concerned that he wasn't showing much loyalty to the team he's a part of—and he's a newcomer. Also, I think that Robert is right. Kristian tends to only use two or three songs during the half-hour set; he sings them over and over again until they become boring. And then, between the songs, he stands there, eyes half open, nodding and smiling as if God and he are having a little chat, while the rest of us look on.

"Perhaps it's better to make good use of the time we've got, rather than steal time from the sermon," I theorized.

Kristian didn't appear to be listening and seemed to think that the more we sing, the happier God gets. "God is looking for fervent, intense worship, Hel," he said, smiling and nodding again like he does between songs. I was worried that, mid-chat, he was going to pop off to some kind of ecstatic place where only he and Jesus can go and that this would lead to an embarrassing lull in our conversation. I also worried that he would call me "Hel" for the fourth time, and so I excused myself and left. He's a little odd, but I'm sure that his foibles could be sorted. What that man needs is a good woman at his side and maybe a short theology course. I'd be happy to help.

I spent most of the rest of today sleeping and dreaming about running the marathon.

I saw Mr. Hemming on the boardwalk this morning when I was running my three miles and waved at him. He didn't wave back; he didn't even smile.

Called Vanessa on the way to work this morning to say hi and casually mentioned that I'm irritated not to be losing weight faster.

"I'm worried about you, Helen. Don't get so caught up that you end up being superficially obsessed about your weight. And anyway, the Bible says that the body will waste away."

"That's my problem," I said. "I'm not so much wasting away as moving into a significant program of expansion."

Agreed to carry on conversation over lunch (must eat fish and chips to impress Vanessa that I care not about the proportions of the flesh).

Yikes. Lord, what do I do? My mother texted me midafternoon and wants to meet my friends from church. The problem is that I don't particularly want my friends from church to meet my mother. I love her dearly, but what if she decides to cleanse their chakras over the roast chicken? She also keeps going on about how she wants to meet "that nice man James that you run that church group thingy meeting with." Sometimes my mother has the tact of a nuclear warhead. I wouldn't be surprised if she tried to marry us right there and then, over the carrots. Still, maybe it would be good for her to be around more "real" Christians. Perhaps they might be able to get through all that incense smoke in a way that I can't.

Vanessa phoned and we chatted some more about the pier crowd.

"What they need is a safe place to just hang out, Helen. A youth club might be a good way to start—how about it?"

I bristled. "Vee, the last youth club we had in town closed down six months ago because there was a terrible fight there. I'm not sure ..."

Vee was insistent. "So, perhaps what was missing was good supervision, Helen. The club idea sounds good to me. Give it some more thought ... I'm praying for you."

"Thanks, Vee. You're a good friend. I was chatting with my Mum the other day about you—I'm so glad you're in my life. She said she'd love to meet some of my friends."

And that's how I accidentally invited Vanessa to Sunday lunch with my parents. "What a great idea! How about next Sunday. Would that work for your mum?" She then said that she would phone James straight away and invite him to come too, as she could tell that I was busy. That girl is such a matchmaker ...

Lord, please don't let my mother make everybody eat with their hands, like she did at Auntie Gillian's last year. Palms are not adequate receptacles for soup. Lord, stay very, very close to me this week. And especially next Sunday ...

I had a thoroughly dull and boring day of back-to-back meetings and then attended a numbing training session about case protocols. The day was punctuated only by fears about the weekend and lunching with the parents. The final nail in the hideous coffin that was this foul Tuesday was driven in when I got home. A letter from Mrs. Hemming was waiting for me. I knew it was from her; she always puts a "God is love" sticker on everything she sends, and she's written to me before, when she and Mr. Hemming resigned from our house group (which was a day of great joy and celebration).

I opened the letter with the sinking heart of a condemned woman, knowing that this would not be good. I was right.

Dear Helen,

Greetings in the unchanging name of our Lord (Heb. 13:8).

I am writing to you today as an act of faithfulness (Num. 12:7, Luke 16:10). I do this with much sorrow (2 Cor. 7:9), but even the deeply unreliable New International Version says that "wounds from a friend can be trusted"—or more accurately, as the King James puts it, "faithful are the wounds of a friend" (Prov. 27:6). I am very concerned about your decision to train for the marathon. Paul the apostle clearly teaches us that "bodily exercise profiteth little" (1 Tim. 4:8) and I am fearful that you are being distracted away from what should be real priority in your life, which is to seek first the Kingdom of God (Mt. 6:33). My fears were confirmed, Helen, when my dear husband informed me that, during his prayer walk along the boardwalk today, he happened (is there such a thing as coincidence? Prov. 3:5) to see you out running. He tells me that he briefly glanced at you as you went running by in your red and blue Lycra running clothes (with blue trim and yellow emblems that fitted very snugly around your bottom) and that while his momentary observation of you wearing such unsuitable attire was ended as he averted his eyes (Job 31:1), he was somewhat concerned that you might be seen by other men in the church who are less mature than he (Phil. 3:15) and then they would be led into carnal lustings (2 Cor. 11:3).

Have you prayed about this? Are you aware that anything that makes others stumble is wrong (Rom.14:13)?

I pray that the eyes of your heart may be enlightened (Eph. 1:18) to see the truth (John 8:32) and that you will truly and sincerely come to the place of fruitful repentance (Matt. 3:8).

I speak as a faithful watchperson of the Lord (Ezek. 3:17) and because I love you in Jesus.

Yours cordially in Christ,
Joan Hemming

My response was to think some of the words that Hayley has taught me in the advanced profanity class that is our relationship.

Finally I saw sense and called Robert. I felt bad because it was late, but he said he didn't mind. I read him Mrs. Hemming's letter, and he sighed a long sigh when I got to the end.

"Helen, some people tell others not to do things because 'they make the weaker brother stumble.' They're not vulnerable, new Christians who are easily offended, but manipulative control freaks who use the stumbling teaching as a way of controlling others and spreading their legalism."

He lost me a bit with that. "So you're saying Mrs. Hemming's wrong?"

"Yes, Joan Hemming is wrong. Period. Health and sports are valuable to us both physically and emotionally. In that passage Paul was simply trying to encourage us to keep our lives in balance and not neglect prayer and the Bible."

"So I can keep running. And I don't have to do it in a parka and three layers of sweatpants?"

Robert laughed. "As long as you're not being provocative, your running gear is fine. Mr. Hemming's problem is his problem and not yours." He chuckled. "I'm gathering from the detailed description Mrs. Hemming has that Mr. Hemming's momentary glance wasn't all that momentary."

Eeewwww.

But although I felt better after I'd chatted with Robert, I felt a bit sad for him after I'd put the phone down. Mr. Hemming is his chief deacon, after all. He may irritate me, but he and his gruesome wife are a constant thorn in Robert's side.

Prayed for Robert and Nola, that God will give them strength. And patience. And courage. I thought for a moment about asking God to kill the Hemmings (slowly), but I'm sure that whole "God is love" thing means I shouldn't.

Wednesday, February 9

I went to see Hayley again this morning. I received a police report stating that last night there was some sort of "domestic" goings-on at her aunt and uncle's. I rang the doorbell about eight times this morning but no one answered. I'm convinced I heard the TV though. However, before I could be sure, I had to remove my ear quite quickly from the letterbox because something on the other side was growling in it. They have one of those psycho dogs who seems to think it's living in some post-apocalyptic nuclear winter, where, in order to survive, it must savage anything that comes along.

I called Hayley's school, but they didn't seem to know who I was talking about. It seems that truancy is another issue that I need to add to Hayley's case file.

God, there must be something more I can do specifically for Hayley. The youth club will be for all of the kids —but what does Hayley need? Please protect her from those who wish to harm her.

Rats! I think I may have a broken washing machine, and if it floods and ruins this flat, I am going to have a fit. I love my flat and have felt great coming home to it ever since I moved in. I know it's not the hugest space in the world, and it only has one bedroom, but I feel perfectly safe and at home here. I used to live in a crummy flat in a rather dubious and scruffy part of town, so my little place near the seafront is a joy.

I have my dad to thank for that. He came to visit me one evening in the rooming house, on a day when I was feeling pretty depressed. The damp in the place had managed to creep up three of the four walls and had even managed to turn my running shoes a strange shade of green. My bedding was actually wet to the touch, and all my clothes smelled like they had been cursed by the bog fairy and left in the washing machine for two years.

My dad came round, saw what a state the flat was in, saw what a state I was in, and offered to help.

"Honey, you can't live like this. Let me give you a deposit for your own place."

I'd like to say that I, of course, immediately refused because as an independent woman I wanted to make my own way in the world without anybody's help, etc. etc. But the truth was that I instantly flung myself down on the floor at my father's feet.

"Yes! Yes! Thank you, Daddy, I'll never be bad again."

Then I jumped up, screamed, and started singing the

only song I have ever composed. It went something along the lines of:

> *I'm getting a flat*
> *I'm getting a flat.*
> *Hold on to your hat,*
> *Helen's getting a flat.*

Hardly the domed cathedral height of genius, but I must admit it was catchy and I sang it in the shower for days.

This flat was the first one we looked at, and I instantly fell in love with it. My father went around knocking on floorboards and unscrewing the shower head whilst I lay down in the middle of the floor.

"Give me this flat, or give me death!" I proclaimed. At which the realtor seemed to back away a little faster than necessary.

I feel so blessed, especially because even though my parents aren't desperately poor, they aren't rolling in money, and it was a big sacrifice for them to do this for me.

Anyway, today I was trying to figure out the troubleshooting section of the washing machine manual that was obviously written by a five-year-old after consuming a candy store's worth of food additives. In the end I gave up and phoned James, who came round right away.

He took the manual from me and scrutinized it. "Ah-ha."

"Ah-ha?"

"Yep." Reaching into the bowels of the machine, he pressed a reset button somewhere. "That should do it."

"Are you kidding?" Suspiciously, I turned the washer knob and heard the sound of water running into the basket. I turned to him in disgust. "How do you do that? How can you take one look at that crummy, foreign-tongued manual, and fix this thing? I spent hours on this!"

James just grinned and waggled his eyebrows. "Not so bad, is it, having a man around the house?"

Was I wrong to call on James like that? I know he came running because of what he feels for me—so I feel a little bit manipulative. On the other hand, he seemed delighted to do it, and after all, a girl needs clean clothes. And what does he mean, having a man around the house? Is that another hint that he'd like to be my permanent man around the house? Yikes.

Thank you, Lord, for James: a very nice platonic friend. May it stay that way, although if you want me to marry him ... no, I can't think about that right now. And, too, thanks for my parents. You've been so good to me. May my mother behave tomorrow. And may she not ask if James and I are an item. And if she does, may James not say, "I'd like us to be." Amen.

What a day!

Went to New Wave this morning as usual. Robert's sermon on prayer was good, especially the bit where he told us that sometimes his mind wanders and he ends up praying for the characters in television soaps to get themselves sorted, which would truly be a miracle. Mrs. Hemming grunted when he mentioned soaps and television and shot her husband a look that gave the impression she'd never heard of such a newfangled and, indeed, worldly invention as a television.

Nola did a solo this morning, which was great. She's such a smiling, calm, normal lady—she works part time as a philosophy lecturer at the local community college. And, blissfully, she's not afraid of Mrs. Hemming, who looked sullen all the way through Nola's piece. Her song was beautiful, not warbling and shrieking like some pseudo-operatic solos in church.

Kristian did a great job in leading worship, although I didn't think it was necessary to sing the refrain of the last song thirteen times, and I wish he wouldn't talk so much between the songs. He seems to have transitioned from being a happy mystic to being a verbose sage. He's still gorgeous, but even more gorgeous when he's being quiet. I was surprised to find that I was too busy worrying about the upcoming parental lunch to focus much on drooling over him.

After the service I chatted with Nola.

"Thanks for the song, Nola; it was really beautiful."

She blushed and smiled. "That's nice of you, Helen. I was a bit worried about that final high note, but I think I just about hit it, although I was standing on tiptoe, and I think my eyebrows were on the top of my head."

"I've been thinking about stretching myself a bit, lately. Vee and I have been worried about the kids who hang about the pier at night, and so we've wondered about starting a youth club. Well, I've wondered, and Vee is praying her socks off for me."

Another smile from Nola. "That sounds like a fabulous idea, Helen — but a lot of work. I don't want to discourage you, but if you start something like that, you need to be in there for the long haul. There's nothing worse for these kids than someone apparently showing them care and then giving up a few weeks later. My only reason for saying that is that I know you're so busy at work, and some of the cases you deal with are really draining emotionally, so I just wouldn't want you to stretch yourself too much. Is there anything that Robert or I could do to help?"

I said I'd give it all more thought and get back to her. I also told her about how I was off to Sunday lunch with Vanessa and James and Mum and Dad and asked her to pray that it would go all right. She winked and said she'd put in some fervent overtime.

As we came out of the church James opened the car door for me, which was nice (as long as he was not trying to impress me with his future-husband politeness skills), and we drove over to Infusion and Vanessa came bounding out, enthusing about their service and insisting that "God had really showed up." I confess to hating the "God showed up" phrase, which makes God sound like an unexpected and disagreeable relative "showing up" for Christmas, like my Uncle Ron with the ill-fitting dentures who came unannounced last year and brought hideous presents and his terrible flatulence problem with him.

When we got to the hobbit cottage, my father met us at the door, wearing the same crinkled suit I had last seen him wear at Great-Aunt Margery's funeral seven years ago. My mother had obviously told him to make an effort for my friends, which was actually very kind of her — and nice of him, too, to be so compliant. I know he hates suits, having been sentenced to wear one in the city every day for decades.

James banged his head on the door frame, as did I, though Vanessa seemed to glide her way effortlessly through. My mother insisted on kissing and hugging us all, even though this was the first time she had met either Vanessa or James. I swear she pressed that boy to her bosom for a little longer than necessary, and he looked like he was going to faint with embarrassment. Vanessa, on the other hand, loves huggy stuff like that, and it was actually my mother who eventually had to pry her off like a limpet.

"Call me Kitty," my mother cooed at them, giving James a saucy wink. "I've opened a bottle of champagne because it's not often I get to meet Helen's lovely friends."

I suddenly panicked. You see, it's the drinking. Neither Vanessa nor James drinks at all. We're talking not even a sip of port at Christmas. I wouldn't be surprised if James even refused brandy butter on his Christmas pudding.

As for Vanessa, I think everybody's secretly relieved that she doesn't drink. Vanessa is energetic enough without enhancement.

My parents however, are drinkers. They're not alcoholics, but if there was no wine on the table at dinner, I'd be worried my parents had been replaced by robotic clones from the future or something.

Vanessa and James refused the champagne, and I was left in a real quandary. If I said no to the champagne, it would make my mother feel bad. I noticed that it was a bottle my parents had brought back from France last year and saved for a special occasion.

Whatever the reason for the special bottle, she had made a real effort and I didn't want to hurt her and yet I didn't want to look like an alcoholic in front of Vanessa and James.

In the end I took a small glass, protesting as she filled it all the way to the top. But it seemed to make her happy, and it's only a glass of champagne, for goodness' sake. James gave me a strange look but Vanessa didn't even seem to notice. She was wandering around the room picking up ornaments and peering into corners.

My mother poured another liberal glass for herself and announced that, despite all previous precedents, dinner was in fact ready and on time. As we walked into the dining room I was blown away. My mum had made a beautiful roast chicken dinner with all the trimmings, lit candles, and had even put fresh flowers and decorations on the table. It suddenly hit me that despite my mum's slight craziness, she's always made a real effort to look after me and be interested in my life; and she shows it by being someone who does all the details. I remember when I was eight I desperately wanted to go as Cinderella to a fancy dress party, and my mother spent weeks sewing frills onto masses of petticoats. Of course, when I got there, I realized all the other girls were wearing crop tops and skirts in bizarre eight-year-old attempts to look like Kylie Minogue, and so I started to cry, asking to go home. She whisked me home, I changed my clothes, and she took me back, with not one cross word about how long she spent on that stupid dress. I think I still have it in a box somewhere.

The lunch spread before us was a masterpiece. We sat down and James was almost drooling. If I married him, I'd have to buy in bulk, because I've seen that lad eat three hamburgers in a row ...

My mother said, "Dig in, kids!" I reached for a serving spoon, perhaps a little hastily because my mother's roast potatoes are to die for, and I was planning to scoop at least six onto my plate before anyone noticed ... when I realized that Vanessa and James were sitting very still.

"Go on," my dad said, smiling around the table, "stretch or starve, we're not shy around here." But Vanessa and James weren't about to stretch for anything—at least, not yet. We hadn't said grace.

We never say grace at home. When I was a child my mother read a book called *The Attitude of Gratitude*. She went through a mad stage of grace-saying and made us hold hands around the table and sing, even in Pizza Hut.

Someone actually stole our breadsticks while we had our eyes closed. We gave up after that.

But not saying grace to Vanessa and James is the equivalent of blasphemy, worthy of a burning. It is *not* done. "Let's say grace," I interjected, embarrassed.

"How lovely," my dad replied, obviously picking up on my distress. My dad's scary like that sometimes; he can read me like a book. "Vanessa," he said quickly, "why don't you say grace?"

Okay, maybe Dad reads me like a book with some pages ripped out. Vanessa saying grace is pretty epic, in the sense that the plague was epic—it lasted a long time, by the end you wished you were dead, and suddenly it answered that wish.

Vanessa gave thanks. This is what I remember, though I think I may have suppressed some of the worst bits in the inner dark rooms of my subconscious:

"Dear Lord, thank you for what we are about to receive [at this point my parents think it is nearly over and start reaching for their forks] and thank you for this chicken, Lord, this chicken that nobly gave its life so that we might live. Thank you for these potatoes whose roots reached deep into your bounteous soil and also gave up their lives so that we might receive the glorious fruits of your overwhelming and constant grace [at this point my father's shoulders started shaking a little]. We thank you for the fair hands of the wise mother who made this feast for our consumption [my mum made a face], and we thank you for the father who presides over this meal.

I pray you would bring blessing and victory into this house. In the name of Jesus, I call out the goodness and nourishment in this food, and I pray that it would course through our veins and anoint our organs before being expelled as waste from our bodies [my father spluttered into a cough] and sent back to the ground from whence it came. In the name of Jesus I rebuke any disease or bacteria in this food, and I pray that all dross would be burnt up with your righteous fire and sent back to the hell to which it belongs. In the name of the Father, the Son and the Holy Spirit, may he reside with us always. Amen.

Everybody paused and we all waited with bated breath to see if she had actually finished, but she had her eyes closed and was mumbling something about being a warrior queen under her breath. At this point my mother, bless her, seemed to have had enough and practically poured brussels sprouts into James's lap in an attempt to get things going.

Despite all that, the rest of the lunch actually went rather well. Plus the Lord may have spoken to me!

"Mum, Dad, I've been noticing that quite a lot of Frenton's kids hang around at the Pier late at night. In fact, one of my clients from work is part of the crowd that gathers down there. They're always drinking too much, and hassling passersby when they've had too much. I think that they just need somewhere to gather—so I'm thinking about starting a youth club."

"Amen!" said Vee, which prompted a bemused eyebrow

raising from my dad, but Vee continued, oblivious: "I feel that Helen's idea for a youth club is nothing less than a dewdrop from the cloud above. I've been praying much about it."

I concentrated on munching my way through my fourth roast potato. My mother turned to me. "You know, darling, sometimes I worry about you; you seem to do so much, what with your job and your church work and marathon training and everything. You do know it's not wrong to give something up, don't you? You don't have to do absolutely everything, dear."

It was such a simple statement, but it really made me think. I do want to do something for those kids, but it's impossible for me to start a youth club with all my other commitments.

Perhaps it would be all right if I stopped doing something.

And then my father piped up: "I agree with your mother, Helen—we don't want you to wear yourself out, so you'd need to look at your schedule. But if you do decide to go ahead, I might know just the place where the kids could meet. There are a couple of disused rooms in the Civic Centre. They're not great—I think there might be some problem with damp—but at least it would be a start."

He offered to make a phone call the very next day and see if he could book them for me. What an answer to prayer!

It's funny because I never thought that the answers would come from my parents. I thought that someone in my church might have a connection, but here I was, right at home where I belonged and my father had the solution. Why do I think God only works in the church and on a Sunday morning?

When my dad described the room that could be used for the club, Vanessa shot me one of her smiley I-told-you-it-was-the-year-of-breakthrough-oh-ye-of-little-faith looks. James smiled too but looked a bit worried. I think he knows what I know: if Mum's right and something has to go, then I have to give up my leadership role of my small group at church. It's the only thing that I can easily stop doing. I've already collected half of the sponsorship money for my marathon, so I can't cancel that. And besides, I'm strangely beginning to enjoy all the running.

James was looking nervously across the table at me when Mum was giving me notice that I had to stop doing something, and his eyes seemed to be pleading with me: whatever you give up, please don't sacrifice the one thing that we get to do together. It's like he could read my mind. I think he might actually love me. I don't know whether anyone's been in love with me before, and I think I sort of love him for loving me. But I don't know whether that's enough.

Note to self: must phone Nola and Robert and ask for advice.

Over dessert, I asked Dad to tell us about his new battle. James had this faraway look and didn't seem interested in listening, but Vanessa was all ears. She asked him loads of questions about it all, which I think pleased him. Apparently it's more of the same incestuous corruption on the council again. There is a big, old, and rather grand building right in the middle of town, which the council wants to sell to a developer who has plans to develop an exclusive health spa in it. The problem is that the developer happens to be a councilor's wife's brother—the very councilor who is leading the charge to get planning permission granted—and he hasn't declared an interest. And apparently his wife even owns half of the development business. It stinks. It's the beach hut debacle revisited.

Dad said that there isn't enough space for things as there is and that this building was supposed to be used for the community. He said it wouldn't cost loads of money to do it up a bit, and it was disgraceful selling a building like that when our local library was the size of Harry Potter's cupboard. But I'm worried for him. When he was fighting the battle of the beach huts, it took a lot out of him. He was passionate about his cause, and yet he ended up losing almost everything.

I worry about his health. He's fine, but he does get so involved with everything he does. And he's not getting any younger.

I pray, Lord, that you would do something about this spa thing. I can't stand seeing my dad hurt and under pressure. Thank you, Lord, for my parents; thank you that they have always looked after me and I wasn't born to some horrible halfwits like Hayley seems to have been.

I pray Hayley will find someone to look after her who is as nice as my parents.

And show me if it's right to give up the small group. And if it is, help James to be okay with it. Amen.

I called Robert and Nola tonight to organize a chat about the small-group leadership decision.

"How about we get together Friday evening?" Robert said.

"Perfect. I can explain where I'm coming from on this."

"Can you give me a sneak peek?"

I told Robert about the youth club idea.

"Wow, that's very exciting. Tell you what—I'll go ahead and let the deacons know you're considering stepping aside from the group. That way they can begin considering the idea of a replacement leader. Understand this doesn't commit you either way; we'll just see what happens."

Monday, February 14

6:30 p.m.

I got a Valentine's Day card and I'm not thrilled. It was a rather straight Christian card (I prefer the funny ones, personally) with a picture of an ocean on the front and the words "Love and Blessings" in overly ornate gothic text inside. It was unsigned, and all that was written was, "Always on my mind—with love."

James doesn't disguise his writing very well.

First I felt happy—it's always nice to receive a card. But then I felt bad because the card was from James. Then I felt even worse because I didn't even think to get him one. But then I realized that was stupid; sending him a card would be leading him on, and that would be a bad idea.

I've read the bit in Leviticus 10 about Nadab and Abihu who were killed because they offered "unauthorized fire to the Lord." I am now a bit worried that my youth club idea might be just that—my own idea and not something from God. An unauthorized idea. Obviously, it's not that I fear being cremated and judged—I just want to do the right thing.

I realize that I don't have to be afraid, that I'm only trying to do something for God and for the kids. But then I think that perhaps what I'm really worried about is giving up the small group.

And upsetting James.

Why is it that it's difficult to leave things? Christians are enthusiastic joiners, but not terribly good at being able to disconnect from anything. Certainly that's true when it comes to actually leaving a church. Years ago, before lovely Robert and Nola came to lead, a family got upset and decided to move on to another church. They were made to feel like fugitives from God and that they were somehow surplus to requirements and that only the pure elect were sticking around—those with a sold-out passion to the vision. Mr. Hemming said very publicly at the time that the church is like a human body and that every healthy body needs a bowel movement. I couldn't believe my ears—suddenly these people who had walked in fellowship with us for years and who had given their time, talents, and money very generously were actually being tagged in that way. I thought of a few waste-product analogies for Mr. Hemming myself.

So I think that, despite these mad fears, I'm going to leave small-group leadership. I haven't absolutely and definitely decided, because I'd like to wait until Friday's chat with Robert and Nola, but that's the direction I'm heading in. And they have been so understanding and supportive so far.

James won't be happy. On the way home from the Sunday lunch at Mum and Dad's I told him that I was leaning toward leaving, and he went very, very quiet. After a ghastly long silence, he then tried to persuade me to carry on and said how much he enjoys co-leading the group with me and how well we work together, which I think is true. But I can't get this youth-club issue out of my mind, and I told him that I need him to help me in my decision.

Vanessa, unusually, was very quiet as we drove back. Perhaps she was praying. Perhaps she wanted to let James and me have space to talk. In the end, James clammed up and folded his arms, making it clear that he didn't want to talk about it.

Oh, the other news is that the big fuss last week at Hayley's house turned out to be a fight over Hayley stealing her aunt's cigarettes. Her aunt called me at the office this afternoon to demand that I talk to her.

I called her cell phone.

"Hi, Hayley, this is Helen."

"Hey, Helen, what's up?"

"Well ... I understand that there's been some tension with your aunt, and I wanted to ask—"

"Before you say anything, Helen, when I grabbed a couple of ciggies out of my aunt's pack, I was really only taking what is mine. I know my aunt and uncle get a big wad of cash from social services for having me live with them, but she rarely ever cooks a decent meal, and I reckon she spends most of the money on her booze. One of these days the old hag is going to light up a ciggie and spontaneously combust, she's so boozed-soaked. And the old bag won't give me a cigarette allowance, so I just decided to help myself, which I think is fair enough—"

"But, Hayley, stealing and then fighting is not the way to handle this—"

"Don't you tell me how to handle things. When I need a ciggie, I need a ciggie, and that's *now*. Believe me, you wouldn't want to mess with me when I need some nicotine. But then, of course, a pansy Christian like you wouldn't understand anything about addictions, now would yer?"

"Hayley, all I'm saying is—"

"Listen to me, social worker Christian. You've already said too much. You never had parents who get out of their heads and then beat seven bells out of each other—and sometimes you—every weekend. You don't know much about life, darlin'. I don't need any lectures from you."

And with that she hung up. I'd say that went rather well. Not.

I spoke to Hayley's school today as well—there was a mix-up because Hayley won't answer to her family surname at school and insists on being known simply as Hayley B. Hence the confusion in the register and an unfounded fear of truancy. At least the girl's getting an education.

Wednesday, February 16

Good small group tonight. We all did a catch-up, went round the circle, and updated each other with our news and prayer requests. Nice. I didn't mention my thoughts about leaving—I'm still one percent wavering, especially tonight, because the group was so lovely and I'm still worried about James—even more so after the Valentine's card.

Over the obligatory cup of tea at the end of the evening, James came over.

"So you got my card?"

I was a bit surprised that he was so forthcoming, especially as he hadn't signed it.

"I want to make it easier for you, Helen, so that you know exactly where things stand between us."

That freaked me out. Was he declaring love and saying I'm always on his mind because I'm probably going to leave the group, and this was a desperate stab at a romance with me? He's never asked me out before, but over the years we've known each other, his feelings for me have always been obvious, which has made it harder when I've not been able to return them. So now it looks like he's upping the stakes and moving in with a Valentine's Day declaration of undying love ... yikes.

I got back to the flat (having gently turned down James's offer of a walk on the boardwalk) and called Vanessa. I was in a bit of a flap and needed to talk.

"I'll be honest, Helen. I think James could be the 'one' for you."

She asked endless questions about him—as well as pointing out some positives.

"What do you like about him, Helen—and what don't you like? Have you prayed about this? Do you feel spiritually compatible? Could you grow to love him, do you think? And remember, Helen, James really works hard in the sound booth at church. And it was great how he not only came looking for Hayley with us but waded into that gang of kids to ask if they'd seen her. He is a man with quiet authority," she said. "He's practical, spiritual, and faithful. And hey, you should be thankful he's not put off by my eccentricities!"

True words—all the more interesting because she's admitting she can be weird at times.

Yikes. Perhaps James is the answer to my prayers for a husband. He's a good man, a good Christian man. But I can't think of him romantically. So now I am more confused.

Lord, it's tangled-fishing-line time again. Please sort me out. Amen.

Joy, joy, joy. A mystery has been solved and I got completely the wrong end of the proverbial stick. The mailman arrived this morning bearing no less than five items of mail for me. One was the electricity bill (a horrifically high winter bill—I must get out more and enjoy the benefits of other people's heating). And then there was an invitation to get one of those catalogues where you buy a pair of shoes and then spend the next twenty years paying for them at fifty pence a week and 1,345 percent interest. The catalogue went straight into the recycling bin.

But the other three letters were, in order of my opening them, (1) wonderful (2) wonderful and (3) hideous. Let's get to the wonderful ones first.

The first was a card—from James. It was an apology card, with the words "I'm so sorry" on the front and an amusing cartoon inside. But there was a long letter inside too, handwritten—and I realized that I'd been mistaken about the sender of the Valentine's card. It was such a lovely letter, I've decided to paste it in here.

Dear Helen

I'm writing today because I want to sincerely apologize for my bad behavior last Sunday. It was so lovely to be able to have lunch with your parents, and I feel like I spoiled the day with my silliness. I've been thinking about it a lot, and I can't believe that I sulked like I did and then even tried to talk you out of what you feel God is asking you to do. I feel terrible!

Helen, I want you to know that I completely respect your judgment about this. I do want to say (without being manipulative, but it needs to be said) that the group would really miss your leadership. You are so beautifully honest, and I think that your being vulnerable liberates the rest of the group to be themselves when we're together. But that said, I really am fully supportive of your new venture, and I love that in the midst of your busy life, you want to do something to help the kids of Frenton. If you decide to go ahead, it would be great if our group could have a little party soon to send you off and thank you.

I'll be praying for the new work you'll be doing, Helen, and I'd be delighted to come along and help out at the club if you'd like me to.

With love and appreciation,
Your friend, James
XXXXXXXXXX

I'm delighted that James is offering to help, although just a little bit nervous about how much love and appreciation he has for me. But he's such a whiz with computers, and he's got a couple of older PCs that work perfectly well for games—he said we could set them up and also perhaps eventually have Internet access, if we could sort a connection.

I think this is a great idea, although I'm a little worried about the Internet idea, as I don't want the youth of Frenton to be hanging out in my club and popping into naughty electronic chat rooms and asking each other what they're wearing.

Anyway ... not only did James *not* send the Valentine's Day card, but he's also cool with my leaving the small group. Hooray and hosanna! This was the card he was referring to at the group last night—now it all makes sense. It doesn't change or solve the fact that James obviously still likes and perhaps loves me, but at least he's not declaring it with passion or trying to make me stay in the group. Of course, this does create an unsolved and slightly delicious mystery—if James didn't send the card, who did?

The next letter (still under the designation of "wonderful") was a lovely card from the deacons, thanking me for my small-group service and assuring me that they were praying for me as I consider leaving the group leadership to start the youth club. Most of our deacons have the attitude that they want to catch people doing something right; they let people know that they're appreciated. I did notice one thing, though—Mr. Hemming didn't sign the card, which is unusual, simply because he's the senior deacon. Oh well. Perhaps he wasn't at the meeting because he had a cold or was roaming Frenton boardwalk trying to catch young female runners out in their beguiling togs.

The third envelope contained (can you believe it?) an anonymous letter. It immediately revealed exactly why there was no signature from Mr. Hemming on the thank-you card from the deacons—he'd probably scurried off home to tell his wife the news of what I was doing, which then led to the most poorly disguised anonymous letter in the history of unkind epistles. It read:

Dear Helen,

I am writing this letter to you anonymously as I think that it is best that you do not respond to me personally or even know my identity. Please prayerfully consider these words as being directly from the Lord and treat them seriously and not with fickle foolishness as the Israelites of old did (Ex. 32:1).

A little bird recently told me of your decision to abandon and willfully cast aside your responsibilities as a small-group leader in our church. I use this popular metaphor of a little bird telling me, of course, only figuratively, as of course I do not converse with animals and the information came my way through a mutual time of sharing with a prayer partner (Eph. 6:19).

I understand that you are taking this step in order to focus on the development of some kind of youth club in the town. I was surprised—nay, horrified —at this news and would like to ask you a number of questions, lovingly.

Have you reached this decision as a result of much prayer (Col. 4:3)?

Did you discuss your decision carefully with some of the elders of our church, therefore submitting yourself to their wise and manly authority (Eph. 5:21)? Scripture speaks of the hireling and good shepherd and the hireling who abandoneth his sheep when something more interesting takes his fancy (John 10:12). Is this perhaps the case with you? And anyway, do you know your heart and motivation in this, for great is the potential for self-deception?

Will this be a thoroughly Christian youth club, where only godly music is played? Will there be a clear and indeed sound evangelistic presentation at the end of each evening?

Will there be a selection of fine Christian literature, with excerpts from Scripture, taken from a reliable translation?

Search your heart, Helen.

Sincerely in Christ,
From one who cares.

PS: God is love.

I was relieved to hear from James, delighted to get the thank-you note from the deacons, and beside myself with anger at what is obviously a note from the Queen of tiresome, Mrs. H. I was considering popping round to their home to commit an act of arson when I decided to return to pondering the other more welcome communications that I received lately. Again, if James didn't send me the Valentine's card . . .

. . . then who did?

Late evening

I think that Robert and Nola are possibly the most wonderful Christian leaders in the world, and we're very lucky to have them in our church, if there's such a thing as luck. I took the thinly disguised epistle of venom from Mrs. Hemming round so that they could take a look—and I thought Nola was going to pop round to the Hemmings' and sort them out there and then. Nola is so quiet, so reasonable, and yet there are times when she gets very angry when she sees religious people doing horrible things, like sending anonymous letters. She became so incensed and animated that Robert smiled and let her talk it all through with me.

"First of all, Helen, I'm so excited about the youth club. You know as a lecturer at the community college I often see kids dropping out of school. It's such a shame. I think that a gathering point for kids is long overdue."

"That really means a lot, Nola. This is a huge thing I'm contemplating."

"Well, don't you even give a thought to Mrs. Hemming's notelet of death. You don't need to feel intimidated by her." She growled in frustration. "Too many Christians have a messed-up notion that 'serving the Lord' is only about working in the church, as if God is a localized deity who lives in the church parking lot. That's not true! God loves his church, and we need to partner with him to see the church's ministries resourced—but most of all he is building his Kingdom. God's out there in the big bad world, Helen, and he's doing his stuff and wants us to get involved. When we care, serve, listen, help out, or surprise people with kindness—the equivalent of the biblical cup of cold water given in Jesus' name—then the Kingdom is built and extended."

"Evangelism is important, Helen," Robert chimed in. "But not everything that we do has to be overtly evangelistic. You don't have to have a sermon, tracts, and Christian music in order to make something that honors and pleases God. In fact, all of that might be thoroughly off-putting and not the purpose of the club at all."

I could definitely see tracts and sermonizing as off-putting to the kids I work with.

"The point is you know the kind of work you need to do for those kids, Helen. When outsiders see life being lived God's way—where people on the margins suddenly matter, where those who have been stereotyped suddenly find a welcome and where conversation and community can take place—then God is pleased. Go for it Helen—we're totally with you."

Robert then said that he was going to have a word with Mr. and Mrs. Hemming. Apparently Mr. Hemming had been in the meeting when my resignation from small-group leadership was announced and he'd sported a face like thunder and then refused to sign the card. Now, with his wife joining in the mad trend to not provide a signature, things had gone way too far.

And, of course, there's a certain irony about their being so uptight about this—namely that they left our small group and don't attend one at all these days. Mrs. Hemming is apparently of the opinion that they are too mature for the kind of trivial sharing that goes on in fellowship groups, which is complete piffle.

"Anyway," Robert concluded, "it's time for the Hemmings to know that this behavior has to stop. I'll stop by and have a chat with them."

Nola smiled. "I'd be happy to stop by as well ... with an incendiary device."

After too many cups of coffee with Robert and Nola, I decided to pop over to my parents' place to tell them about Mrs. Hemming's poison-pen letter. Robert and Nola are marvelous, but sometimes I just need to hear my dad's perspective too. He's my biggest fan, and even if he only says what I already know, there's something about the way he says it that always make me feel better.

Mum was out for a girly night at the movies with her friend Babs, and Dad was reading a Russian novel that weighs about thirty pounds. He gave me the hug he always gives me, as if we've been apart for months or years. I love it. I told him about the unlovely Hemming epistle and he shook his head in disbelief at her maliciousness.

He said, "I'm so sorry you have to put up with her sanctimonious and cowardly madness, darling. Anonymous letters have always been a thorn in a lot of people's sides. Apparently D. L. Moody, the famous evangelist, was preaching one time when someone decided to send him a vitriolic unsigned note during the sermon. The nasty little message was passed across the pews to an usher, who took the folded note to the pulpit and placed it before Mr. Moody. When he opened the note, Moody found that it had only one word written on it: Fool. 'I've just had the oddest note,' Mr. Moody said to the congregation. 'I often get letters where people write the letter but then forget to write their signature—but in this case, the person forgot to write the letter and just signed their name.'"

I like D. L. Moody. I love my dad.

I'd love to know who sent me that Valentine's card.

Saturday, February 19

Managed eight miles today—the training is going well. I feel so much better now I've finally made a decision to move on from leading the group. It does seem to me that Christians sometimes overcomplicate decision making. Sometimes you have to make a decision and trust that God will sort it out, as opposed to spending so long waiting for a booming voice from heaven that nothing gets done.

Katy is going to help James with leading the group, so a replacement for me has been found already. I'm still waiting to hear from Dad about the room for the youth club though.

Laura and I went out to a club tonight with some other people from work. As we sat there, I realized that my friends are so different. The thought of Vanessa and Laura actually ever having a conversation or even being in the same room fills me with dread. They are simply from different planets. And yet both have strengths in different ways. Laura is a survivor. And she's got an uncomplicated straightforwardness about life that's refreshing. Sometimes when I get into the paralysis of analysis, she'll come up with a blunt stun-grenade sentence like: "Oh, get over it." Her uncomplicated approach to life means that, every now and then, she'll make such a statement—so wise and yet so stupidly obvious.

I was bold enough to confide in her the other day that I do feel guilty quite easily. Her response was as obvious as Mrs. Hemming's bottom in Lycra, but it stopped me in my tracks.

"Look, Helen, this Christian stuff you're into is about forgiveness, right?"

"Yes, it does tend to be a large part of the Christian gospel."

"So, if you've messed up, sort it with your God and then move on. If you're going to believe that stuff, you might as well believe it all, including the good bits."

Wise words indeed. And yet Laura does have a very obvious blind spot. She's having relationship problems with some creep called Dave. Apparently he's all "intimate" with her in private but ignores her in front of her friends. It doesn't sound like he likes her much, but she seems smitten.

I told her to ignore him for a bit, because I'm sure that's what you're supposed to do in that situation, not that I've had much practice. The funny thing is that, even though he's treating her badly, I'm kind of jealous. Maybe if I don't compromise, I'll never find anybody?

Why is it that Laura seems so full of common sense,

but when it comes to Dave the dirtbag, she can't see that he's using her? And why is it that, when it comes to life, I have so many questions?

Lord, I pray for my future husband; I pray that'll you'll keep him safe for me and keep the nasty roaming hands of other women *off* him. I pray that he'll be completely and utterly in love with you, like I am. I love you. Night-night.

Sunday, February 27

Horrors. It's been ages since I've had a time of journal tapping.

Mad at work.

Church this morning was great—one of those mornings where everything seemed to be perfect—almost. Robert's sermon on becoming a servant was excellent, not least because he acts like one and so happens to be a walking, talking illustration. Kristian did well with the worship—it was sane, accessible, and inspirational, and he kept to the allotted time. I smiled at him when he sat down. He smiled back, those baby blues flashing.

Not only that, but I noticed that during Robert's sermon, Kristian was nodding and definitely taking notes— no songwriting for him today. Perhaps I've been too harsh with Kristian. We need to give each other space to grow.

Still no news from Dad about the room for the club.

Tonight Nola invited me round for a cup of tea, and I found myself in the unusual position of having to cheer her up—which is odd, because it's nearly always the other way around.

"I'm so discouraged, Helen." Nola's normally bright eyes seemed clouded, and I think she'd been crying, if her puffy eyelids were anything to go by. Perhaps she's not been sleeping well.

"The Hemmings are so destructive. I'm really struggling with them. It's not great to have murderous fantasies about members of the congregation—even less deacons and their wives! Robert went to have a chat with them this afternoon, and it didn't go well—actually, all hell broke loose. Robert began their meeting by thanking them both for their years of service in the church—he's so good at trying to bring the positive—but then mentioned the letter you received."

I immediately felt grateful for Robert defending me and confronting the Hemmings—even though I knew it would be an unbearable meeting.

"Robert told Mrs. Hemming that people who write letters should have the courage to sign them and that the church leadership should either totally get behind efforts to impact the community or at least disagree with grace and kindness. At this point Mrs. Hemming exploded. I've never seen the movie *The Exorcist*, but I can imagine that, if Mrs. Hemming was fifty-five years younger and sixty pounds lighter, she could do an outstanding head-revolving/bile-spitting/fingernails-growing-six inches-in-three-seconds act to produce a devil worshipper.

"I can't believe that woman, Helen. At first she even denied sending the letter until, in the end, her husband blew her cover by saying that he agreed with what his wife had written, which was unfortunate. Apparently she shot him a look that suggested that he is going to greatly suffer when they're next alone. That man is probably never ever going to experience carnal relations again. Sorry, Helen, did I really just say that?"

I wrinkled my nose and smiled. It was a gross thought.

"Well, if that did happen, Nola, it would serve him right, because it would be a just reward. Those two are just bullies."

Now I was working up a real head of steam. I was angry at getting the letter and angrier about Nola being distressed by those two.

"That's what they are, Nola—Bible-toting bullies who get their own way with a subtle violence that might actually be uglier than a punch in the mouth. And they're cunning with it. One of their weapons is the catch-all criticism. If someone does something that they don't like or would not be their personal choice, they can attack that person, not by using Scripture to justify their arguments but by simply playing the you-make-me-stumble card. And when they do quote the Bible, they simply seem to bruise people but not shed any light on their issues."

Nola nodded. She'd usually be uncomfortable around the straight-shooting talk that I was indulging in, but I think she was relieved that I was putting into words what we both knew: the Hemmings are mean.

"Then there's the unity/division/rebellion cards that they use, Nola. If anyone disagrees with Mr. Hemming's leadership on the deacon board, then he cries foul by saying that the person who disagrees is threatening the unity of the church with their 'divisive' comments. You can't ask them a question, because anyone who tries to challenge them is tagged as being rebellious. No, they're not being rebellious; they've just got a brain cell and would like to use it. So, what happened once Mr. Hemming gave the game away and let Robert know that his lovely wife wrote the letter?"

"Oh, she finally admitted it but never did get around to apologizing for lying. And then she had the gall to bluster on about how her words were hard, like Jesus' to the Pharisees and Paul's to the Corinthians, but they had to be spoken. She said she isn't responsible for God's standards, and she was worried that the good name of the church might be smeared if it got out that someone from the fellowship was running a youth club that was not absolutely Christ-centered."

There's something horrible about actually hearing that someone is criticizing you and accusing you of something awful, even though Mrs. Hemming's letter had already made that perfectly and painfully clear. I thought about replying with a sentence that included the phrase *vicious cow* but thought it might be a bridge too far.

Nola paused, like she was trying to hold back tears. "Mrs. Hemming ended the meeting by switching tactics and turning on Robert. She said it was his lack of sound teaching from a proper translation of the Bible that had helped create all this chaos. And then she played the ultimate hand: she said that he, the leader of the church, wasn't deep enough and neither were his sermons, what with all those silly little anecdotes and humor. Why, she said, Jesus didn't laugh, did he?"

Nola said that the meeting ended up with the Hemmings virtually kicking Robert out of their house—but they didn't threaten to leave the church (which would have probably given rise to the throwing of an instant street party). Instead, Mrs. Hemming yelled that they were not alone in their concerns, that a good number of folk in the church were troubled.

And then the knockout punch: they said that Robert should seriously pray about his future ministry at New Wave. The message was obvious: "We're not leaving and you might be. We can make it happen. We were here before you came, and we'll be here after you've gone. This church is ours. Remember that, Robert."

Nola couldn't hold back when she talked about it. She started sobbing, and I decided that I really despised the Hemmings.

As I passed Nola a Kleenex I realized that I wanted to hurt the Hemmings. And then I realized that, in rightly calling them bullies, I could resort to bullying tactics myself. Nevertheless, they are wrong. God help me to keep my attitude clean and avoid ending up like them.

Do I love the Hemmings? No. Am I willing to love them? I'm not sure. Do I feel like loving them? No.

Nola and I ended up resorting to watching a chick flick together. More tears, this time from both of us, but this time because Colin Firth got the girl.

The great news is that I got a phone call from Dad.

"Darling, sorry it took me so long. But we got the room, and we can use it for a year at a token rent."

I squealed. "Daddy, you did it! I can't believe it!"

"Now remember, the room's not much to look at, but it's a start."

"It'll be just fine. Seriously. James is willing to lug the computers in and help with setting things up, so I think we're on a roll. Oh, wow!"

I couldn't believe it was actually going to start happening. I was also instantly overwhelmed at the thought of the loads of work ahead of us in setting up the club.

Dad changed the subject and mentioned the battle with the council over the proposed sale of the proposed spa building—it's called Lawrence House—was heating up. He's trying to get a public meeting organized.

I could sense his frustration. "I'll pray for you, Dad." And I certainly would.

Saw Hayley, who was much the same and suggested that I might like to shove my head where the sun doesn't shine, which of course was not a reference to Alaska during the long winter months.

A wonderful thing has happened. What with the news yesterday from Dad about the room for the youth club, today's terrific happening is turning this week into a fabulous time of almost apocalyptic proportions (not sure this is the best analogy, but it certainly is a good week!). Stand by and hold on to something solid because the news is that Kristian Vivian Rogers, worship leader and love god of this parish, called me today and asked me out! Yes, I kid you not.

But there's more ...

"So, Hel, did you get the card?"

My brain fogged over a bit. "The card?"

And then ... "The card!"

He was the one who'd sent the Valentine's card!

Of course I did ask him outright about it, in order to avoid any further confusion. He confirmed he was the sender. Thank you, Lord!

"Actually, I didn't realize it was from you. It didn't seem to be your kind of style."

"Yeah, I was in a hurry that day. Just dashed into the Christian bookshop and grabbed the first V-Day card I could find."

Okay, so this ever-so-slightly niggled me, but I managed to stifle it because *I AM GOING OUT WITH K.V. NEXT SATURDAY FOR COFFEE!*

Vanessa is right. This is a year of breakthrough.

Popped into the Civic Centre to see the room Dad has gotten for the youth club—and he's right, it's not much, but we should be able to put a pool table and a Ping-Pong table in and a few tables with computer games, courtesy of James. Add a few music DVDs, and at least we're off to a start.

Wednesday, March 2

It was such a lovely, lovely evening at my final night as a small-group leader. People said some very nice things to me—I am far too embarrassed (and humble) to write the details of them down here. Why is it that I am so good at taking criticism to heart, but struggle when people say nice things about me?

One person after another took turns to thank me and say what my leadership has done to help them, and then they prayed for me and the youth club, which was fantastic. Although I did have one tiny niggly thought about that when I got home—more about that in a moment.

Then James announced that the group had decided to take a little offering to help the club on its way—and they gave me an envelope with £679.27 in it! I am so excited. In fact, it's far more than I've raised so far for the marathon.

Back to my niggle (why do these weird thoughts come to me?), which is about the way that we do prayer. You see, we spent about thirty minutes in the group talking about the club—people asked me questions, and I tried to explain as best I could what I felt we wanted to achieve —and then we spent the next twenty-five minutes telling

God all the things that he'd heard us spend the first thirty minutes talking about. I know that prayer matters—and the prayers tonight came from people who not only love me but put their hands in their pockets as well—but I'm not sure that we always get prayer right.

I didn't tell James about my upcoming date with Kristian. I'm not sure how he'd be with it. Will try to do so soon. Hate the thought of hurting him.

Friday, March 4

My sunshiny blue-sky day was marred a bit because I had a confusing lunch with Vanessa today, and we actually had a bit of a mild row—the first disagreement we've had in absolutely ages. I told her about my date with destiny tomorrow, hoping that she'd be thrilled for me, but she was the opposite.

"Okay, so I've only seen Kristian in action once, and ..." She frowned.

"And?"

"I wasn't impressed." Seeing me ready to retort, she held up her hand. "There's a subtle difference between worship leading and performance. I felt that Kristian was a bit too impressed with himself."

"He's just confident!"

"Hmm. Okay, how about after the service when he was holding court with some of the younger girls in the youth group? Everyone else in leadership was praying with people at the front."

"Well ..." Okay, I didn't have an answer for that one. Which ticked me off.

She shrugged. "I don't feel at peace about you getting together with Kristian. Just my opinion."

"I respect your opinion," I said stiffly. "But I also respectfully disagree."

Vee gave me a long look, and I'd swear she was privately praying over me and my—in her opinion—bad decision. "God only has one person alive on Planet Earth who is chosen to be your partner, and you can't miss the best or compromise." And with another shrug she went back to eating her lunch.

Didn't know how to respond, and I think I defended Kris with a little too much fervor. What that means is that I was close to yelling at Vanessa and telling her that I didn't care what she had peace about. I'm hoping that Vanessa is wrong.

But then she confused me by insisting on the whole "one partner on Planet Earth" thing. Thinking about that for a bit tonight, I can't see how that works. For one thing, I can't find anywhere in the Bible that says that there's only one person you can marry. And then, what if you marry someone and they die and you marry someone else —was the second person being held as first reserve until the other one died?

There seem to be some good biblical reasons why a divorce sometimes happens. So what if you have a biblical divorce and then you marry someone else—are they a reserve candidate too?

Didn't come to any final conclusions, but decided once again that I must be willing to question some of the ideas that we Christians pass around to each other without thinking them through first.

Anyway, none of this is going to spoil tomorrow. Oh happy day to come.

Saturday, March 5

Woe and thrice woe. Kristian and I met at Marinabean, and right from the beginning I knew that things weren't going well. For a start, he was late—thirty minutes late, in fact. He didn't even apologize about keeping me waiting.

He bustled in, a huge and immediately irritating grin on his face, like he'd just accomplished something great rather than kept me waiting.

"Wow, Hel. Good to see you. What a day I've had! I just got totally lost in God's presence as I was composing this morning."

I waited for him to ask me how my day went, but the question never came.

"Composing is such an intense, beautiful thing, Hel. I'm not sure if I can communicate the depth of it to you … you're not musical, are you?"

"No, I'm not musical, but I am punctual," I said, and stunningly, he didn't get my rather unsubtle barb at all.

He just got up, went over to the counter, and ordered a complicated double shot with vanilla cappuccino (the most expensive drink available), then asked me what I wanted, and headed for the bathroom without a word, leaving me to get up and pay for both coffees. When he came back, he didn't even say "thank you" and made some snide remark about fair-trade coffee being a big waste of time. This was not going well.

"Well, I think fair trade is certainly not a waste of time, Kris. Every small step makes a difference, and we have a responsibility, not to just sing songs about changing the world, but to take actions that follow through on the songs …"

He didn't seem interested in listening. And then, without responding to my comment or asking anything about me, he launched into a further long, boring description of his morning. Apparently, he likes to take every Saturday morning out to pray and compose.

I sat there wondering why this man had sent me a card telling me that I was on his mind. He didn't seem to have room there for anyone apart from himself.

Anyway, I digress. According to the delayed-and-fair-trade-despising Kristian, the Lord and he have cozy little chats when he spends time in solitude and picks up his guitar. Apparently a guitar is a conduit for some sort of special holiness.

And then, incredibly, he said something like: "Hel, I was writing this worship song this morning, ya know, getting into God's presence, and I had this image of rushing water, ya know—powerful but cleansing. And I felt that

God was telling me to write a song about it, like he put the lines straight into my heart. And I wondered what you would think about it, Hel ..."

He then launched into a speech about how he wanted my "input" because he had not only felt a strong spiritual connection with me, but also because I was beautiful. That made me feel a little better—for about a minute. He also said that he was not consulting with the worship backup singers, because he didn't feel the same connection with them in the Spirit. I was flattered at first and then managed to engage brain and decided that I didn't like the way this little chat was going at all.

But then Kristian rounded up his monologue by launching into an arrogant tirade about what he calls "yesterday's worship leaders." He said that he was one of the fresh voices that God was raising up with a new DNA, to connect totally with the angst in today's culture, and that many of the more established worship leaders were "yesterday's people who were tired, old hat, and should make way for the new thing that God was doing. What is needed are real pioneers," he said, "who will take risks."

I couldn't help thinking that some of those veteran songwriters and worship leaders had taken huge risky steps in their lives in a church culture that had been far less open to change than church is these days and that Kristian was lobbing a bunch of real pioneers into a Dumpster. But I kept quiet, mainly because I couldn't get a word in.

Then it got worse, because Kristian shared the words

of the song that he and God had written this morning. Here's a brief excerpt as best as I can remember it:

> Rushing water flow, flow,
> I am so lowly,
> Love me slowly,
> Jesus. Jesus. Jesus.
> Let your gentle water wings cover me,
> Engulf me worshipfully.
> Jesus. Jesus. Jesus.
> You are the King-River of my heart.

I was speechless, which is rare for me.

I hope that he doesn't try to introduce it into our church, because one run through that little ditty and the entire congregation will be on a conference call with a suicide helpline. Hopefully, lovely Pastor Robert is far too sensible to allow Kristian to share this twaddle.

But then I realized that I had a big problem that I've bumped into before. How do you disagree with someone who claims God has told them to do something, when it's obvious that he hasn't? If God gave Kristian that song, it was probably because God didn't want it in the first place. But when someone prefaces everything with "God told me" or "the Lord spoke to me," then that's it—discussion over.

It reminds me of a conference that I went to last December on prophecy. Someone stood in the last service and loudly declared, "Thus says the Lord of hosts: a very merry Christmas to all my people." It was obviously mad

—but they'd already decided that God was telling them to do this. Is "God told me" sometimes a term that insecure people use to cover their tracks—or even a way to manipulate others into agreeing with them?

At the same conference, someone else felt the urge to spontaneously lead the gathered congregation in a song and launched into "He'll be coming round the mountain when he comes ..." This all went swimmingly until we got to the "Singing ey, ey, yippie, yippie, ey" bit, whereupon it died a fast death.

I do have a real problem with Kristian because I'm starting to think that he's a bit of a pompous, self-obsessed drip, but I am still attracted to him. A lot. His musical drivel is obnoxious and off-putting, but those blue eyes and blond hair and even now slightly faded tan are still very nice indeed. I'm confused.

That's it. I fancy him a lot and don't like him today at all. Vanessa was right.

Sunday, March 13

Good run this morning. Managed to cancel out thoughts of death and cardiac arrest by doing some serious thinking about youth-club plans.

After showering I managed to read my Bible. I've only read four chapters this week, all from Jonah. I've always thought the story was about a large fish, and ever since watching Veggie Tales, I can't read this story without thinking of Jonah as a prophetic asparagus. But I was struck by how furious that little veggie—I mean prophet—got with God. He was in a real hissy fit and told God so. I wondered about some of my polite speechlike prayers—some of which perhaps contain lies if I don't tell God what I feel.

Okay, God. What I am about to say may give the impression that I am a very bad Christian. But reading Jonah has taught me that it's a good idea to tell you what's on my mind. I don't want to be judgmental, but it's hard enough to get people to believe in you without people like Mr. Hemming sticking terrifying leaflets about hell in people's faces.

During church this morning Robert was reading out the usual church notices: Would anyone like to volunteer for church cleaning ... The worship practice is on Tuesday nights ... Would people please ask for permission before they stick anything up on the notice board ...

Robert rather pointedly looked at Mrs. Hemming when he mentioned the notice board, which I suspect might be a reference to the leaflet advertising a conference called "The King James: The Bible Paul Used" that was pinned up anonymously.

To be honest, I wasn't concentrating. I was actually pondering the vital issue of what color mine and Kristian's children's hair would be. My biology is strictly Key Stage One, and I was trying to remember about recessive and dominant genes. Since I have dirty blond hair and he has blond hair, there is a good chance we would have lots of beautiful blond-haired cherubs who might look mildly

Swedish despite hailing from Frenton. And they'd tan beautifully. How cute would that be?

Obviously my mid-service fantasizing means that I have decided to forgive Kristian for his idiotic self-obsessed behavior during that disastrous date. Time heals; it's been a whole eight days since it happened, and he did look utterly gorgeous this morning. Not only that, but he didn't try to teach his King River song to the church, which gives him points in my book. If he asks me out again, I will ponder, say that I'll need to think and pray about it, and will let him know in a day or two ... and then will magnanimously say yes.

Anyway, I digress. At the end of the announcements, Robert asked if anyone had any other items to share. Mr. Hemming took that as an invitation to stride up to the pulpit.

"I need to pass on a message from the Lord to the congregation."

Okay, that hardly constitutes an announcement.

Poor Robert's face was a picture, but before he could protest Mr. Hemming grabbed the mic and was off. He launched into an impassioned rant about how God had called us all to be evangelists and we needed to take our responsibilities more seriously and that he was already leading the way by standing outside the local Tesco's on Saturdays, handing out booklets to passersby. He was waving one around while he talked, and it had flames on the front. *Flames!* And not only flames, but I'm sure I saw a little picture of a devil with a pitchfork as well ...

Something tells me that this booklet isn't awash with

good news. If anyone asks me why I'm a Christian, hell is the last issue I would think to talk about. I'm a Christian because of Jesus, not Satan. Why tell people about hell when you can tell them about heaven? Am I wrong? I don't know ... another thing to talk through with Nola ...

Anyway, Mr. Hemming's "winning" technique is apparently to point his finger at poor unsuspecting shoppers and bellow, *"You are lost and you are going to the abyss!"* in their faces.

He finally finished his angry "invitation" to others to come and join him for the Saturday morning evangelistic mugging. Strangely, he didn't have any stories about anyone actually converting. He did say that the devil did try to stop his good work by demon-possessing a homeless man, who kept asking him for change. But apparently he rebuked him in the name of Jesus and the man wandered off.

Sometimes I think Mr. Hemming doesn't get it, but then I think, if Mr. Hemming doesn't get it, maybe I don't get it either, seeing as I don't think I've converted one single person in my whole Christian life. Nor has anyone ever got better when I've prayed for them, at least from any epic illnesses. I've prayed when people had coughs and colds, but never knew if they recovered quickly because (a) the cold ran its course, (b) they nuked it with cough medicine, or (c) a congestion-battling angel of the Lord was dispatched because of my intercessory efforts. Option (c) doesn't seem that likely.

Last year I prayed loads for Mrs. Malone, who was dying of cancer, and I believed she would be all right. But she still died. Perhaps I don't believe in God enough. But how can you tell; it's not like you can measure faith with a meter, can you? And how does that work out with God anyway? When he heard my prayer, did he say, "Mmm. Helen has 91.45 percent faith, but in order to spare Mrs. Malone from a painful death, Helen needs to get that faith level up to a minimum of 96.34 percent ... Sorry, Mrs. M., it's time for you to get hooked up to the morphine drip and prepare yourself for a painful demise."

I must ask Nola about all of this.

Lord, please help my unbelief.

I'm confused about the heaven and hell and healing and faith thing. In fact I'm confused about lots of things. But I am certain I don't want to adopt Mr. Hemming's techniques. I've decided that Mr. Hemming might be like Jonah, who preached loudly but hated the people he preached to. And I'm not sure that it's a good idea to call people lost. They are lost if they don't know God, but surely that's not the end of the story, is it? The fact that God sent Jonah hotfooting it to wicked Nineveh means that he was desperate to find people—he's the good shepherd who goes hunting for his idiotically wayward sheep.

So perhaps a better term to describe people who don't know God is sought, not lost, because there's a God who urgently wants them to know his love ...

All this threatens to make my head explode. Okay, some good news: Robert caught me after the service.

"The deacons have voted to buy a pool table for the youth club." He paused. "Not unanimously—there was one vote against."

Surprise, surprise.

So things are coming together. We're still a way off from being able to open, though. Once we start, I want us to be open consistently, every Friday night for starters, so I've decided to wait until after we get back from our annual church trip to Together for the Kingdom, a big Christian music-and-teaching weekend that they hold in the north. Tens of thousands attend. It starts on Friday and ends Tuesday evening.

Vanessa is really excited about it. She says it reminds her of some of the big Christian festivals in the USA, like Jesus Northwest, but she also loves that the emphasis of Together is more on teaching and worship than it is on performance music. And it's very interdenominational too. We've got a group of about sixty going, and Robert and Nola are coming too, which is lovely. I'm so glad I can call them my friends. Our last minister had told everybody that he would be "shepherd of all and friend to none" because during his training he'd been taught to have no favorites. But Robert has made it clear in his teaching that we all need friends and he wouldn't live under that kind of prohibition.

Robert and Nola are both very wise—strangely, they're a little like Laura, but Robert and Nola know where their wisdom is coming from. It's more than common sense. They know God and they know their Bibles. And they're kind and ordinary and all 'round nice human beings that I'd like to be like.

Roll on, Easter.

At work Laura had the distinct misfortune to pop into Tesco's for a loaf of bread last Saturday and told me that she'd met a very odd man and asked me if he was from my church. I coughed and mumbled something about not being sure if he was—which is terrible! I denied even knowing Mr. Hemming, which is a lie ...

After work met Mum for coffee in Marinabean, and then we spent a lovely couple of hours meandering around the stores.

"So, darling, any men on the Helen horizon at the moment?" It's a question that Mum asks me at least quarterly. I decided not to tell her about Kristian, as I'm really not sure if that's going to go anywhere. So I blathered on about James's lovely letter of apology and my ongoing niggle that God would insist that I marry him.

"Surely it doesn't work that way, does it, darling? Didn't God invent love, and so the usual way that people get together is because they realize they love each other, rather than responding to a divine directive to go forth and multiply?"

Sometimes my mother makes absolute perfect sense.

Lunchtime

I can't believe another whole week has gone by. I've been working hard on my running, which is going well. I had a nice coffee catch-up with Vanessa last Wednesday, and she told me that they are having a special interdenominational healing service at Infusion tonight, so I'm going along.

Church was good again this morning. Robert spoke on the power of love from 1 Corinthians 13 and said that the famous chapter was far more than good material for fridge magnets.

Kristian led worship well. I'm glad I decided to give him another chance last week, seeing as Jesus has given me about a billion other chances, but Kris still hasn't asked me out again. I tried to catch his eye a couple of times this morning, but without success.

After the service I talked to James.

"I'm excited but a little apprehensive about this healing event at Infusion tonight, James. Are you going?"

"I am, Helen; in fact, the whole of our home group is tagging along. What are you worried about?"

"Well, I think it's because I don't need any healing—and so I'm wondering if I'm just going along to view some fireworks—it all seems a little voyeuristic. And I've been to a few of these events before, and frankly, I didn't like them—they seemed like circuses to me. And so I'm not sure I'm going with an open heart."

James smiled.

"That's one of your great strengths, Helen—you really want to get it right. But I wonder sometimes if you get yourself tied up in the paralysis of analysis. I think you can be too hard on yourself. Why not just go along and see what happens?"

I really liked James for saying that—and then a small cloud appeared as he told me that Kristian had found out about the event and had asked if he could tag along with the New Wave crew, which James didn't seem too thrilled about. He said that the outing was an opportunity for the small group to bond a little and, as Kristian is not in the group, that it wasn't a good idea. Then he said that despite this he didn't feel like saying no to Kristian, which I was glad about because I felt quite excited about spending some time with him again. I also thought that James has forgotten that I'm no longer in the small group, so the bonding argument doesn't wash ...

Anyway, I'm glad that Kristian is coming. Perhaps he had been horribly embarrassed about that appalling date and has been trying to summon up courage to ask me out again. Grant him boldness, O Lord ...

Just before Bed

My, what a night. I met Vanessa outside the school that Infusion rents for their meetings. She was carrying a "prophetic sculpture" that she'd made for the evening, which was basically an assortment of twigs that were plugged into a base of bloodred-painted clay, with a single daffodil atop them. It was very large, one could not ignore Vanessa's work, even if one wanted to.

"It represents the leaves for the healing of the nations," she said.

Okay.

There was a guest speaker — a rather odd evangelist chap with very strange hair who is planning to come back to Frenton later in the year to hold what he called a "crusade." Wondered if this involved people dressing up as medieval warriors and then galloping along the boardwalk in search of heathens to convert, impale, or both. Mr. Hemming would like that ...

The service, to be honest, was awful. Got the distinct impression that God was in dire need of persuasion to heal, seeing as this evangelist prayed at an earsplitting volume.

People who were prayed for were asked to immediately declare that they were healed, which was both embarrassing and heartbreaking. Weird Hair shoved a microphone in the face of a girl who'd asked for prayer for a stutter and gleefully announced that she'd be able to speak perfectly. Cue loud applause and cheering from the congregation. All went rather well, at least for a few words. Then she said, "I'm really grateful that Je-Je-Je-Je-Jesus has he-he-he-healed me," which is when the clapping stopped. I wanted to cry for her.

Then the fiasco got worse. A chap with something wrong with his knees was prayed for, and then he was told to run up and down the platform. This he did without too much hobbling, which prompted more clapping, though it was more nervous applause this time. Thrilled that he'd finally got something close to a result, the evangelist demanded that the chap with the healed knees do a victory lap around the hall. He dutifully obliged, but unfortunately got excited as he came steaming up the centre aisle like a bat out of he ... heaven. Sadly he didn't notice Doris's handbag, left in the aisle. He tripped, went flying, and broke his ankle, becoming perhaps the first person to be taken to the ER from a healing service.

But it was during the singing of the last song that the most embarrassing event in the history of the universe happened.

I noticed that Doris's handbag had been kicked onto the platform by the sprinter with the knees, and she needed her glasses to be able to see the song words on the screen. Because she couldn't see the words, she was singing "la, la, la, la, la" at the top of her voice like an elderly out-of-tune Teletubby. I thought I'd retrieve her bag for her, but I hadn't noticed that the wooden floor had been liberally splattered with the olive oil that the evangelist had used for the praying ...

I yelled "Oh God!" at the top of my voice as I skidded and slid my way across the greasy floor; someone took this to be urgent intercession and shouted "Amen!" very loudly. I then smashed into Vanessa's prophetic tree and the leaves for the healing of the nations were scattered all over the platform, like it was suddenly fall season. Finally I found myself face down on the floor, looking like I was prostrating myself in worship before Mr. Evangelist Weird Hair.

But then a certain sense of discomfort overcame me. A physical discomfort. And I realized ... In the course of my tumble, my skirt had ridden right up my back and my scarlet-red thong was now on full display to everyone.

Oh Lord, indeed ...

I staggered to my feet, conscious that a few people in the crowd were giggling and one or two actually stuffing Bibles into their mouths. James rushed forward to help me up, but then, as I turned around, I noticed that Kristian was giggling too, and he had this rather stupid leer on his face.

I am starting to not like him again now. I punctuate a Christian gathering with a prophetic sculpture collision and then flash my underwear at everyone, and he thought it was funny. Not nice.

At last the service ended, we cleaned up the oily tree branches, had a terrible cup of tea, and headed for home. We gave Kristian a lift, and he talked endlessly about how he'd had prophecies that he was going to take his music to the nations of the earth, that he frankly felt more at home in the large setting of Infusion tonight, and that he was born to lead huge crowds in worship. He also ripped into the poor lady who led the songs, because she had us sing a couple of older worship songs and even a hymn.

I couldn't help thinking about poor deaf Doris, who was sobbing her way through "Amazing Grace." Her deafness means that she yells everything, and over the appalling cup of tea I overheard her bellowing that she'd sung that hymn on her wedding day and at her husband's funeral, so it meant a lot to her.

I was wrestling with the temptation to break Kristian's guitar (he calls it his harp) over his head (he'd taken it with him tonight, even though he wasn't leading worship, because he says it's an emblem of his God-given identity). The more he went on, the more I wanted to hurt him. But then, bizarrely, I'd still like to kiss him as well. I am sick in the head ...

Oh, nearly forgot. Mr. and Mrs. Hemming also showed up at the healing service tonight, and she ranted over the mud-colored nasty tea about how she'd only attended the event because she was suspicious that unsound teaching was being proclaimed. As a "watchperson of the Lord," as she described herself, she was gravely concerned because her worst suspicions had indeed been confirmed. And she glared at me, which served as silent confirmation that she'd been unimpressed by my unfortunate collision and the mildly indecent exposure that followed.

My problem is that she is probably right—the evangelist chap taught that suffering comes when we don't exercise enough faith and that he is supernaturally exempted from sickness because the Holy Spirit warns him that suffering is coming, like a heavenly air traffic controller. I'm no theologian, but I know that's tosh.

So what with the healings that were probably iffy and then the way Awful Hair murdered Scripture in his preaching, Mrs. Hemming might be right ... and yet, she's wrong. She may be correct and orthodox, but her attitude stinks. She was sniping at a greater volume than poor old deaf Doris, but she never once went up to the visiting evangelist (who looked like he was praying over the dish-water tea to try to make it drinkable — without success, from the look on his face). I remembered Robert's sermon from this morning, when he said that if we don't speak the truth in love, then we don't speak the truth. Remembered, too, how Mr. Hemming had loudly barked "amen" at that point in the sermon and then turned around and glowered at everyone in the church, as if to say, "You lot need to hear this." What about his acid-tongued spouse who was parked next to him?

Anyway, back to Mrs. Hemming's "Tonight's preacher was unsound" speech at the healing service. She got on a roll, until James finally wandered over to her to say hello. More to shut her up, really. Small talk seemed the best way, but James said that Mrs. Hemming continued her earsplitting rant about the evangelist and the evening. He made his excuses and we fled.

So now, I'm off to bed and I feel a bit depressed. We Christians are supposed to love each other, but some are tough to even like. Kristian is not only more and more irritating, but also irritates me more because I'm still vaguely attracted to him. It's not his fault, but I feel like blaming him anyway.

James is lovely, and it was nice that he came to rescue me when my thong was almost wrapped around my ear-lobes, but there's still no spark.

As for the Hemmings, words fail me. I wish that words would fail them.

I'm exhausted. Need sleep. Need faith. Goodnight.

Truly a few days from hell. I started the week feeling a bit morose after the healing service debacle. Perhaps the only good thing about that disastrous evening is that it's unlikely that the evangelist is going to hit Frenton with a crusade now.

I had to go to see Hayley again yesterday, and her dislike of me has now become more and more obvious. She hinted her irritation by opening the door and telling me to go forth to another place swiftly (won't write down what she actually said, but I think I learned a couple of new swear words today).

She wasn't finished. "I hate your guts; I wish you'd get into a terrible and fatal car wreck and be burned alive in the gasoline-fueled flames. You've done nothing to help me out."

"Listen, Hayley, I'm doing the best I can," I bristled.

Whereupon she said, very slowly, "Well done." And she actually gave me a slow hand clap.

I'm quite good at my job, and I'm normally confident enough, but I wanted to burst into tears. Instead I bit my lip.

Lunch with Vanessa didn't go so well either. She didn't seem to be listening (and that's so unusual for her) when I told her about my desire to gag the Hemmings, and about Hayley, and even that I wanted to punish Kristian a little for his smirking (but would end up kissing him instead). She rattled on about how her prophetic tree had been shattered by my little oil-based trip, but how it was no accident. There are no coincidences, she says, just Godincidences. Everything therefore means something. But I can't get my head around that at all. God doesn't plan everything—and everything doesn't have a purpose, does it? Little children are abused and trafficked and God doesn't plan that, does he? Got exhausted thinking about it, so gave up. Looking forward to getting away to Together for the Kingdom.

Dad called and said that he'd managed to get a great deal on a brand-new Ping-Pong table for the club, which he and Mum are going to donate. At least things are coming together in that area of my life. I'm planning to open the club around four weeks from now. Need to recruit some more helpers. Also need to do endless forms, checks, admin, etc., etc., all of which is boring and time-consuming, so I am not going to waste more time by writing about it here. I will be glad when it is all over! Robert has arranged a work party of people from church on Saturday to clean the room up and paint it. I love Robert and Nola.

Friday, March 25

The bad news is that I think I may just have been sexually assaulted by a Scottish terrier dog. It may have something to do with the fact that, because of all this exercise, I no longer resemble an overstuffed sausage in my Lycra gear. I'm no chipolata, but I definitely look better than I did before! I don't seem to be driving men blind with desire (still no invite to another date from Kristian, which may be a good thing), but I do seem to be having an alluring effect on small animals.

I was running in the park this morning, mumbling prayers under my breath. I began praying for my friend Laura's miraculous conversion, but the prayer quickly turned into more of a gasping plea for God to please, gasp, make my lungs stop burning like a fire in a paper factory. Then who should I right smack into but Kristian!

Whilst grabbing onto him, gasping and trying to apologize at the same time, I noticed that his eyes were all red, like he'd been crying. I asked him what was wrong, and we ended up sitting on a bench for forty minutes discussing his pain. Apparently things haven't been going too well for him; he'd been getting some vibes of criticism about his worship leading style, and he was beginning to wonder whether New Wave Christian fellowship was the right place for him after all.

I felt slightly put off by this, because I so love our church.

He started talking about how he feels that God has given him all these dreams about influencing the whole world with his songs, but that no doors are opening and he feels trapped in the small backwater that is New Wave.

I felt a mixture of sympathy and irritation about that, but then came the mad-dog attack. The assault came from Barnabas, Kristian's Scottish terrier. He's definitely a cute little thing (the dog, not Kristian. Well, and Kristian ...), but during the whole conversation, in which I was trying to pull that sympathetic and wise "I am your friend; let me offer you profound and spiritual advice" face, Barnabas was (as Barry White would have put it) trying to make sweet love to both of my legs at the same time. Kristian was so caught up in his own misery that he didn't seem to notice, and I kept trying to shake the poor thing off without looking like I had some sort of problem. After a while, it all got a bit much, because Barnabas was going at me like a jackhammer. So, with a little more violence than I intended, I suddenly kicked my leg out, which flipped the dog up into the air (he did a rather impressive triple somersault) and landed him sprawled and stunned, yelping and whining like the rejected lover that he was.

Kristian gave me this appalled look as if I should immediately be arrested by the Humane Society for my obvious cruelty to animals. And then he asked if that was necessary, and then he started to cry again. The poor man really does love his dog.

I felt so bad that I offered to buy him coffee on the condition that Barnabas was left outside. We went to Marinabean and actually had a good time. He bought the coffee —progress!

We sat down at my table (well, it's not actually got my name on it, but you know what I mean).

"Things with the youth club are going well, Kris. We have a work party from the church to clean up the room tomorrow." I braced myself for a wall of noninterest like before. And I was thrilled that, this time, Kris was different.

"That's great, Helen. It sounds like an exciting project. I'll come by for a couple of hours tomorrow, if you like —I'm rubbish with a paintbrush, but I can help with the cleaning. And then, when everything's up and running with the club, I could come in and lead some worship for you if you like."

I thanked him for the offer of help with the cleaning —but managed to avoid getting into the idea of a worship session at the club because I can't imagine some of the kids I know singing songs about rivers and mountains. I can imagine them stealing his guitar and giving him an education about some of the finer points of the songs of the rapper Fiddy Threepac, whose most recent single was entitled "Head-Stamping" ...

Then I meandered on about my hopes for the club, and he actually listened and asked some intelligent questions too! A definite improvement.

Spoke to Mum on the phone tonight. She said Dad's been working flat out on fighting the spa proposal and that he's trying to pull a public meeting together so that people can air their views openly. I hope he wins this one.

Saturday, March 26

I've had the strangest day. I phoned James this morning and told him about how Kristian is discouraged and could use our prayers, but he didn't seem too concerned and made some comments about Kristian needing to live in the real world and get rid of some of his head-in-the-clouds ambition. James is usually very caring, but he obviously isn't too keen on Kristian, which is a bit sad—we can all change and grow.

Then I went straight into town after my run along the beach, a run where I nearly surrendered both my ears to frostbite despite wearing the red woolly hat my grandmother knitted me when I was thirteen. I had decided to buy a book by this guru guy Bshach Yabba so I could engage in what I hoped would be an intelligent theological debate with my mother.

The hope is that I will say some incredibly profound things and she will realize she has made more than a few deeply illogical errors, tear out her crystal nose ring (though hopefully not too violently), and declare that Jesus is Lord. Then she will rebuke Bshach Yabba in the name of Jesus and sob on my lap, begging for forgiveness.

This seems to be a running theme in my Christian fantasies.

I decided to go to a rather junky-looking bookshop down Penny Alley because it has a reputation for selling quirky books. I ducked in, careful to avoid my reflection in the shop window, as I'd rather not be reminded that my red hat was clashing beautifully with my bright-pink face. Not to mention that my Lycra jogging gear made me look like I was smuggling saddlebags and two small bags of flour. I might be thinner than I was, but am not yet thin enough and the eating lapses of this last week haven't helped.

The guy behind the counter was slouched in a chair, his legs propped up on a desk, his head immersed in a copy of *Thus Spoke Zarathustra*—you know, that bizarre book written by Nietzsche, who declared that God is dead. Anyway, I made a halfhearted attempt to try to find the *Chakras and Sacrifice* book before I got bored staring at endless rows of book titles, which were called things like *Wearing Derrida's Mouth-Guards: Speaking Before You're Spoken To* as well as the surely riveting *Philosophy and the Abyss: Transgressing the Crevice* and the potentially intriguing *God, the Dirty Dancer of Death*. I decided to ask for help.

At first I tried to attract the attention of the shop assistant in the classic British way—where you stand still and occasionally glance nervously at the salesperson. When that didn't work, I decided to move a bit closer and stare at him more fixedly, even clearing my throat and shuffling round a little. However, he was completely and utterly engrossed in his book. I tried to catch his eye, but all I could see was a head of long chestnut curls and so I was finally forced to ask him for help.

"I would happily help you, madam," he replied, his head still buried in his book, "but how do I know you actually exist? You might be a figment of my imagination, something dreamt up by my senses to play with my mind."

I paused, because, to be honest, I didn't know what to say to this. If I knew I was going to be forced to engage in philosophical debate, I'd at least have brushed my hair and put my reading glasses on. They make me look and feel more intelligent.

"Listen," I finally replied, "could you help me find a book called *Chakras and Sacrifice* by Bshach Yabba?"

He still didn't look up. "Absolutely not, because that

book is a pile of guano. A waste of time. Trees were cut down needlessly to produce that useless book."

With this he finally looked up and ...

"Aaron?" I said.

Yes, it was Aaron, my boyfriend from college days. He looked slightly different now with long hair (to be honest, it suited him much more than that horribly boring crew cut he used to have at university), but it was him all right. He was wearing a black polo-neck and black jeans, with those ridiculously long pointy shoes that are back in fashion, also in black—I think they're called Winklepickers.

"Hi, Helen!" he exclaimed and then babbled a nonstop stream of questions and answers without pausing for breath. "It's been ages. Why on earth are you trying to buy a book by Bshach Yabba? Have you given up on the Christian malarkey? Well, you won't find any answers there. I've looked. All I got was a sprained back from all those positions that Yabba insists that you contort yourself into."

I looked confused. Well, in fact, my confused face is also my "I've just had a disturbing thought" face, as I momentarily considered Aaron in a variety of contorted positions.

"You know, from the yoga," he explained.

"Oh," I said, relieved. "No, the book isn't for me; it's for my mother. Well, at least I'm reading it for my mother. She's got into the chakra thing, you see, and I wanted to find out what it's all about so I could help her."

"Right. Still dancing the Christian fandango then, Helen? You were always so much better at it than I was. You were a natural, whereas I always felt like I didn't know what I was doing, like I didn't belong. I used to hand out all these leaflets and go to all these Christian events because I thought that's what Christians did, but it never made me feel like a Christian, or at least what I thought feeling like a Christian would feel like ..."

I had absolutely no idea what to say. I mean, I hadn't seen the man for years and here he was jumping right in and telling me his deep, spiritual problems within seconds of saying hi. In fact, I'd just realized that I hadn't actually said hi. Plus, this was the man who had actually dumped me for not being holy enough. I managed a rather fake sounding "oh dear" which came out of my mouth and sounded like sarcasm, though I did mean it in a kind way. I felt bad for him. But "oh dear" was the best I could manage. There was a long silence that felt like an hour.

"I like your hat," he suddenly blurted out and moved into another machine-gun monologue. "It's very retro, makes you look like you're from the seventies. Wow, I mean, I wish I could be in the seventies now. There seemed to be so much more energy back then."

How would he know, I wondered? He wasn't born until the eighties!

"People seemed to care more about stuff. Have you been running or something? You look all pink. It's nice — healthy looking. I don't do much exercise anymore. Sometimes I just lie in bed for days."

He sighed, but he didn't just sigh, he put his whole body into it. It felt like the sigh took about two minutes, during which I once again blurted out "oh dear." Then I actually felt like I wanted to sigh too but had to hold it in because I was worried that he might think I was mocking him. Which to be honest, I was now seriously considering doing. I felt sad for his sadness but a bit bemused by the strange, odd bloke that he had become.

"Good book?" I asked. Not that I cared, but I wanted to say something, anything to break the now incredibly awkward silence that was creeping between us. He didn't seem to hear my question but kept staring moodily into some middle distance. I had to keep stopping myself from turning round to see what he was looking at.

And then suddenly he spoke again. "Do you like Nietzsche?"

"Ummmm, sure, I haven't really read much." I blushed; this was not going well. He was the weirdo, so why did I suddenly feel like a class-A idiot?

"It's good. Really good. You should read it. It's very poetic. But it's dark; it makes me shiver, you know, when I'm alone. But there's something very powerful about it. Very honest."

"Oh dear," I said yet again. I am truly the world's number one thicko. I felt like someone had removed my brain and replaced it with bits of carpet fluff. I wish I read more books. Nola's great like that. Her knowledge as a philosophy lecturer means that she would know exactly what to say in a situation like this. Instead, do you know what I did?

I panicked and asked him out for coffee. I asked Aaron Byrne out for coffee! I have no idea why I did it. It seemed to rise out of my subconscious like vertigo.

"I don't drink coffee these days," he replied. "I drink gin."

"Oh," I said again, "that would be fine too."

I am a complete and utter moron. Mentally challenged mice have higher IQs than me. Anyway, the long and the short of it is that I am now committed to going for a drink next Saturday night with a man who not only dumped me, but who now also seems to be several sandwiches short of a picnic. In fact he seems to have replaced the picnic with a pack of menthol cigarettes, a bottle of gin, and an addiction to weirdness. God, how on earth do I get myself in these situations?

Having asked the man who dumped me out for a drink, I turned and fled the shop. And I never did get that Yabba book. I went in there to try to help one mildly confused person—my mother. And now I've invited another massively confused person into my life, in the shape of Aaron. I'm now confused myself.

But pleased for some reason, because Aaron said yes.

Spent the afternoon at the youth club scrubbing and cleaning and painting ... wasn't sure anyone was going to turn up, O me of little faith ...

Kris worked really hard at cleaning the windows, which were gleaming by the time he got finished. Yes indeed, real improvement all round.

You can now call me Helen of Troy Sloane. Apparently, I am so fair and lovely that men everywhere are fighting over my hand. My face could probably launch a thousand ships, full of men ready to fight for my favors ...

I should explain. At church this evening we had a special worship service, which basically means you cut the sermon time in half and end up waving your hands about with a little more enthusiasm than usual. At some point I think you're suppose to cry or laugh and have a bona fide religious experience—perhaps one of the ones that makes you want to live up a pole in the desert, wearing nothing but a loincloth and filth. Kristian was on stage per usual, white teeth gleaming in the special lights he had rigged up to make the evening more "inviting" for the Holy Spirit.

Personally I think if the Holy Spirit decides to turn up somewhere, he doesn't give a flying doodah-dash about mood lighting. I hope not, anyway, because he's the One who brings healing, and hospital wards don't tend to have dimmer switches and lighting effects.

Anyway, Kristian was in the middle of this loooooooooooooong speech, which seemed to involve him saying a lot of things like "We have to open ourselves fully up to God, caress his face, and love him deeply like a lover" while at the same time playing E minor over and over again on the guitar. Just when I thought that things were going well with Kris, as soon as he picks up his guitar it all goes wrong.

God, I'm not sure whether it's wrong to say this, but

here goes: sometimes worship songs sound a bit, well, physical. I think it's weird to have a whole church singing things like "I want more" or "I want to stay in your arms."

Lord, I know our relationship with you should be intimate, but the way these songs sound, sometimes I'm not sure whether I'm supposed to follow you or kiss you. I hope I'm not saying anything really blasphemous. Maybe I feel like that because I have a horribly corrupt and perverse mind. But what happened to all the songs with an actual story? No one ever seems to sing about characters from the Bible; no one even seems to sing about the miracles Jesus did or the stories he told. Instead, we go on endlessly about the fact that he loves us so much.

Anyway, Kristian was midsentence, when suddenly the sound started going funny. It was strange because the sound never goes funny at church, which is pretty much due to the fact that James is in charge of it, and when James is in charge of something, it never goes wrong. He's fantastic with anything electronic; it's like he has some sort of postmodern techno-gift from God.

So Kristian's speaking in that mildly hallucinogenic worship leader's voice, and the PA starts shrieking and screaming and doing that thing that makes everybody violently clap their hands over their ears and yell because it makes their back teeth hurt. Kristian didn't know what to do, since the deafening feedback completely ruined the atmosphere he had been carefully creating for the last twenty minutes. Kristian muttered something that no one heard because by now the PA was off. He had a face like thunder as he ended his "set," as he calls it.

Robert got up and handled the whole situation beautifully. Strangely, as soon as Robert took the microphone, the PA came back on again, minus the screaming feedback.

"Folks, often we only notice those who serve us technically when something goes wrong. So let's give a hand for our faithful sound engineer, James."

James flushed bright red with embarrassment.

After the service James came to me and quietly asked me to pray for him—I thought that perhaps he was mortified about the screaming banshees in the sound system. And then he confessed something terrible to me.

"I'm a bad person. I was so sick and tired of Kristian and his prima-donna attitude and his pretentious ambitions, I deliberately cranked up the PA in order to hijack his 'set.'"

"Wow." I was a little bit shocked but a little bit delighted too. For once, dutiful, responsible James had done something risky. And I think he did it because he's jealous of Kristian and the fact that I like him. Okay, it was very naughty of him, and he certainly shouldn't have disturbed the worship like that. But I laughed all the way home when I thought about him doing that and then getting a congregational round of applause for his faithful service thirty seconds later.

So now I have James getting edgy and naughty because he wants me, and Aaron wants to drink gin with me (and that means he wants me), and Kristian is perhaps coming to his senses and is realizing that he wants me too. Life is looking interesting . . .

I've eaten virtually nothing all day, due to nervous energy expended about my date with Aaron tonight. Which is crazy because I'm not even sure this is a date—and if it is, I'm not sure that it should be or that I want it to be, and *I am so confused!* Decided to go with the flow and try to enjoy the evening. Aaron is so totally strange it might be high in entertainment value.

6:05 p.m.

We are going to a poetry-and-music night in a newly opened rather trendy café near his bookshop. It's not Covent Garden, but for Frenton, it's about as on-the-edge as it gets. Apparently, poetry has changed Aaron's life. Poetry has also momentarily changed my life because I am now in a state of blind panic, as I'm unsure about what exactly one should wear to a poetry gig—a beret and a striped top perhaps? That might look like I'm mocking, but what if I turn up in something completely inappropriate and everyone realizes that I'm just a boring Christian with absolutely no handle on the bohemian underbelly of Frenton?

I managed to shave one leg before realizing that the razor was almost totally blunt, so that at least means skirts are out of the question—don't want Aaron to think that he's out on the town with the Yeti.

I have found my top, done my hair, and am wondering, why am I making such an effort? He's practically a card-carrying atheist, from the sounds of it.

Lord, please help me to be stunningly profound tonight so that Aaron will instantly believe in you again. I mean, he did it once ... how hard can it be?

Sunday, April 3

It is not April Fools' Day—that was two days ago—but guess who is the fool ...

I must write this to try and get my feelings straight about last night. It was such a blur of emotions; I'm not sure exactly how to feel about it. What I do know is that I feel very, very bad.

Let me put it plainly: last night's little outing with Aaron was a terrible idea. It pains me to remember the details ... but remember I must.

I met Aaron at the café—I was about ten minutes late. He didn't seem to mind but the poetry reading had already started so I had to sneak in quietly. As I tiptoed towards his table, I tripped, and the guy on the open mic gave me a very pointed look and sarcastically thanked me for paying attention. Aaron stuck his tongue out at him, which made me giggle, and I received another dirty look. He had already bought a bottle of gin—although, since he produced it from his inside jacket pocket, it probably wasn't from the bar. I hate gin, so decided I'd wait to order a coffee in the break. We sat back to watch and listen.

Each act was only allowed on for ten minutes and even though some of them were awful, there were a couple that were actually all right. The MC was very funny, and the audience kept heckling in the background. Aaron either enthusiastically applauded or muttered "Philistine" under his breath and kept whispering rude things about the performers in my ear. I never realized that he could be so funny. It made me think that maybe we should heckle in church a bit more; it might liven things up, but then I thought about what would happen if Mr. and Mrs. Hemming were allowed to heckle.

Aaron seemed to be drinking quite a lot. During the break I dashed up to get coffee. Then we went outside so that Aaron could smoke. By the time we got back in, there was only one chair left. I went to offer it to Aaron, obviously keen to show him that Christians aren't all bad and some actually offer their seats up for others, but he sat down on it and, in one quick swoop, grabbed me round the waist and plonked me on his lap.

I haven't sat on a man's lap for about three years. I tried to imagine James doing the same thing to me and the improbability of it gave me the giggles, which made Aaron poke me to be quiet, which of course made me giggle even more. It took me a while to compose myself, during which a young girl got up to read some actually pretty good poetry.

I realized I had already been sitting on Aaron's lap for some time and thought it would be rude to get up now. Besides, Aaron was comfortable, and I felt very secure as he had one arm around my waist to stop me from falling off. As the show ended, I excused myself to go to the bathroom, where I learned that the toilet seat was, in fact, much further down than I previously thought, and as a consequence, I think I have a rather attractive bruise on my left buttock.

I decided that I, Helen Sloane, had not had this much fun in a long time. I went back upstairs, where the crowd had thinned out a little, and Aaron pulled me over to this little corner table, all shadows with some candles flickering, and we started to talk ... and talk ... and talk. The café was beautiful and different; someone had written poems all over the walls in large italic script, and now some angst-filled woman singer was pouring out her heart through the speakers and the lights were down low. Aaron and I could have talked all night—at least that's how I felt. It seemed we discussed everything we could ever think of. Aaron told me all about Nietzsche and some of the books he'd been reading. And he told me about his now not being a Christian; he said that it wasn't that he didn't believe in God any more.

"In a way, I wish I didn't believe because it would make life much easier for me." He paused. "I really never felt like a Christian, and to be honest I have no idea what kind of person I would be if I was one. But I don't think I'd like myself very much if I became the kind of Christian I grew up thinking I had to be."

"Yes! That's exactly it." And the thing is I did completely understand him—or at least I did last night. "Sometimes I feel like I'm living in two completely different worlds," I continued, "with completely different rules, and I have to be two totally different people, and it's exhausting! And all I can think is, I don't want to morph into Mrs. Hemming when I'm old and grey. It's all very well and good proclaiming that you're some sort of spiritual warrior on a Sunday morning during a worship service, but you hardly feel that holy when you're up to your eyes in paperwork and you've got deadlines to meet."

Aaron nodded vigorously, and I ended with a thump on the table. "The church says pray and things will change, but I said that when I pray about work issues, like Hayley, then nothing ever seems to happen."

"Who's Hayley?"

I started telling him what a little brat Hayley was and about how I was trying to help her but she didn't appreciate it and how I'd felt like I'd prayed all I could for her but nothing had happened.

"Cut her some slack, Helen. These things take time."

Hmm. He seemed to be on her side a bit too much, but I tried to be open to his explanation.

He said, "Sometimes it can take years for someone to change, deeply change. Christians always seem to expect instant transformation — especially for themselves — thinking that God will hit them like a strike of lightning and turn them into Mother Teresa overnight. Maybe that does happen sometimes, but mostly change is hard work. The hard work shouldn't scare us, though, because perhaps that means it's more lasting."

Aaron took another huge slug from his gin bottle and started messing around and doing impressions of some of the people in the Christian Group at university. We talked about how they were always calling meetings to discuss some spiritual crisis or another, which was actually much ado about nothing. Aaron admitted that it was actually at one of those meetings where he began to lose his faith.

"Remember when the CG was going to boycott the Spring Ball because the organizers had hired a palm reader who was to be parked in a tent outside the dining room? They thought this was completely unacceptable and that either the Ball Committee should get rid of the tent or there would be a ruling that meant that no members of the CG would show up at the Ball."

I did remember a big hullabaloo about that.

"Okay, so that was fair enough, but I suggested that instead of either not going, or getting rid of the tent and making everyone angry at us, we should set up a prayer tent next to the palm reader and see who had the most effect."

It was at that point that he realized that most people in the group didn't seem to believe prayer would actually have any measurable effect at all—that prayer was something that Christians did because it was right, not because it was effective and potentially life changing.

"But think, Helen. If Jesus had sat in that tent, there would have been a queue stretching halfway around the building!"

It's obvious that however much Aaron has fallen out of love with Christians, he still is a big fan of Christ—at least at a distance.

"But here's the rub. Helen, even though I suggested the prayer-tent idea, I would have been scared stiff to sit in it

—and why is it that in a CG of hundreds of people, there was not one person who seemed to think that it might be an exciting, dynamic thing to do? We are called to be Christlike, but it seems to be so hard that nobody is even coming close. I'm angry at God for making it so easy for us all to fail . . ."

I think he said some more angry stuff, but by that point, I realized that for the last five minutes I had been fixated on his moving lips and thinking about what it would be like to kiss them and trying to remember what kissing him was like a decade ago.

Suddenly he announced that the café was in fact kicking us out. With my mind still somewhat focused on the idea of kissing, I suggested that we go back to the bookshop and have a nightcap. It had started to rain, and by this time I was feeling decidedly lightheaded. On the way to the store, which wasn't far, we were twirling our way round lampposts reciting some stupid made-up poetry. Or at least I hope Aaron was making it up.

It happened halfway through Aaron yelling out, "I'm so high, in the sky, oh why, oh why, I want to crrrrrrry . . ." We happened to be whirling around the same lamppost, and before I knew it we were suddenly leaning against a brick wall outside the bookshop, engaging in some majorly heavy kissing. We are talking major passion here, major. He certainly never kissed like this when we were at uni —because if he had, I would never have forgotten it.

Aaron suggested we go inside for some peppermint liqueur he'd picked up whilst picking grapes in France, and before I knew it, we were sitting on the sofa in the back room. And that's when either God or Aaron saved me from doing some very unhelpful things.

We were midway through a conversation, and I think I was rattling something about how I was so fed up with church, not to mention that horrible letter from Mrs. Hemming. I was saying that I completely understood feeling angry about how difficult being a Christian is and that it's awful when you seem to try so hard all the time yet end up messing everything up. And suddenly I felt completely overwhelmed and hopeless in a "what the heck—what's the point in trying?" kind of way.

And that's when Aaron got to his feet and said in a slight slur, "Time to get you home, Helen of Troy."

He helped me retrieve one of my shoes from under the sofa, hauled me out the door, and walked me home.

Then he kissed me on the forehead, told me I was very lovely, and staggered off down the street.

I must erase all memories of this man from my brain. For starters, he is not a Christian. But then again, what kind of good did I do him? This is the man who dumped me the last time I got drunk, and then a decade later, I meet up with him, he's retired from faith, and I pour out all my troubles about church and morality and Lord knows what else ...

I must have an incredibly cold shower and clean the flat. And I must stop smelling the sweater I wore last night that still smells of Aaron.

It's been a whole week and I still feel bad about last week-end and Aaron and my dumping all my frustrations with church on him. If anything, he's probably thinking that I'm another good example of faith gone wrong.

Church mostly good, although Kristian led worship but then opened his mouth in between songs and shared twaddle. Am definitely off him again now.

Then I had a lovely lunch with Mum and Dad—but she started on about Bshach Yabba again, and that reminded me of how I'd bumped into Aaron. Sad that Aaron hasn't called, but rather glad he hasn't called too because that would potentially make things difficult. I decided to try to distract myself from my issues by quizzing Dad about the Battle of the Spa—he's still plugging away trying to call a public meeting but has come up against all kinds of internal resistance.

I can't decide if Dad is now someone who believes in dark conspiracy theories, or whether the council really is as ridden with corruption as he suggests.

James talked to me about which computer games we should make available in the youth club. I said that I thought it would be helpful if we could have a selection that didn't require drive-by shooting, drug-deal exchanges, or running people over and gaining points for doing it.

Together for the Kingdom, the big church conference, is coming up soon, which is good, as I am hoping to use the space to gain some sanity. One other piece of good news—Katy has volunteered to help at the youth club, which made me glad and sad. I've always had her tagged as a slightly airheaded dancer at the church—and here she is wanting to help me out. I am judgmental and generally all-round bad.

Sunday, April 17

Another whole week gone by and I feel a tiny bit better about life, but not much. I know that if Aaron hadn't taken the initiative to get me out of his flat when he did, then I was vulnerable, in my hopeless state, to just about anything. And he was the one who had been drinking, so I should have been modeling self-control. All the Bible verses I found about sexual sins and wayward women didn't help—a concordance is a terrible weapon when you use it against yourself. I actually plucked up the courage to talk to Nola about my disastrous Aaronic date. She was kind and understanding and said that, while I'd been foolish and could have placed myself in a vulnerable position, I should be grateful that Aaron was a gentleman. I'm sad that, out of the two of us, he should get the award for the better behavior.

I have a totally crazy week coming up as I have to get ready for taking off for Together for the Kingdom next weekend, which means that (a) I need to make sure I buy a new and incredibly attractive arctic thermal gear usually worn by people who hang around with huskies and cook with walrus fat, and (b) also need to get a slimline small

Bible because, although chugging around from seminar to seminar with my huge Amplified Version might have calorific advantages, it is too much effort.

I'm looking forward to it. Some people knock these big Christian events and tag them as unreal, escapist jamborees, but for me and so many others, they're a great opportunity to recharge the batteries, enjoy the excitement of worshiping with thousands—and also graze the gazillion books and CDs available. There are certain dangers, however, and not just from the cutting breeze that blasts in from the North Sea. One's eyesight can at times be in danger from low flying flags wafted by overenthusiastic flag and banner wavers. Our church is not into flags in worship, except for one lady who sometimes stands at the front with a morose-looking face while swishing a ribbon backward and forward with the flair of a windscreen wiper. Hopefully, the Lord appreciates her waving at him. Whenever I see her, I think of that verse from the Psalms somewhere that says that the army of the Lord is terrible with banners. She's certainly terrible with a banner ...

The other slight danger can be overload. If you're not careful, you can dash from workshop to celebration to seminar to debate and end up with a head and heart so stuffed with ideas that you feel like you're mentally constipated. I love words, but Christian events can make me feel like I'm being buried under an avalanche of ideas and, after a while, the words don't mean anything at all. That's why I try to get off-site at least three times over the weekend and go and do anything that's just ... normal.

Kristian is going and shared last Sunday morning that he's written a couple of new songs in the hope that "the Lord might give him a platform for wider exposure." Sometimes when he talks like that, I feel like pushing him off of a platform in front of a passing train. But then I feel like I'd like to rescue him just in time and sweep him into my arms. How confused can a girl get?

James is going too and, true to form, is volunteering to help in one of the venues with the sound equipment. He's also the person who collects the booking forms for everybody and books the cabins at the event. This is good, not only for the eternal purposes of the Kingdom of Heaven but also as, hopefully, he will be so engrossed with all his serving that I won't see him too much, which means that things won't get too intense. And that's good because, these days, he seems to look at me with a "I know what you've been up to" look. Perhaps it's my imagination.

Speaking of James, in his capacity as group organizer, he handed me a sticker for my car today that says "I'm going to Together for the Kingdom," which I'm supposed to slap on my back bumper. I am having a very minor crisis about the application of this sticky appendage, as it seems a bit odd to announce to other drivers where you're going, as if they care. Not only that, but the sticker has a dove on it too, which announces that the driver is a Christian. And when I'm driving (hideous confession coming), I'm not sure that I always want other drivers to know that I am Christian, especially if I've just cut them off. I gave up stickers when I decided to remove the "In the event of the rapture, this car will be driverless" sticker back in 1999 because (a) I don't think I believe in a rapture, and (b) if there was one and suddenly drivers were snatched from their vehicles, I don't think that other drivers would be terribly interested in sticker reading, but would be more preoccupied with avoiding wildly swerving and out-of-control cars.

I decided to forget to put the sticker on.

I'm hoping that Vanessa will be vaguely sensible at Together for the Kingdom too. She loves these big events and always goes absolutely ballistic in worship when she's there. This can be somewhat startling for those who come from smaller, quieter churches, especially when Vanessa moves into high gear. She does this rather strange charismatic dance thing where she twirls round and round while hopping up and down and punching the air, which makes her look like she is absolutely desperate to use the loo and/or has just won the soccer World Cup.

Vanessa also takes a stack of what she describes as "worship accessories" along. These include a rain stick, ten packets of incense, some maracas from Brazil, and a large map of the world, which she has laminated so that she can stand on the various countries while praying, although Israel (for which she likes to pray a lot) is a tough one—being so small, she has to stand on tiptoe.

She'd also like to take her large oil drum with her. Sometimes during intercession at her church's prayer meetings, she daubs her face in rainbow-colored face paint, Braveheart style, and beats the living daylights out of this empty oil drum, which is painted red for some symbolic reason that I forget. But thankfully, the oil drum won't fit into the car. I pray that the Lord never provides her with a trailer.

Nola and Robert are going, which is nice because they'll have the chance to listen themselves rather than them having to give out.

And hooray, Mr. and Mrs. Hemming are not going, predictably, because, as Mrs. Hemming says loudly every year, these interdenominational gatherings are hotbeds of compromise.

The Hemmings have been a lot quieter since the difficult meeting with Robert, but I think it's the calm before the storm—something is brewing. Mr. Hemming tried to insist that he preach in the church while Robert's away at the conference, and (so Nola told me—she probably shouldn't have, but there you go) Robert said that, considering the recent difficulties, this would be inappropriate. Mrs. Hemming waded in (the first time she's actually spoken to Robert since the showdown) and tried to add her not inconsiderate weight to the argument, but Robert stood his ground and refused. Well done, Robert.

Monday, April 18

Bumped into James in the coffee shop at lunchtime, and he asked me if I'd applied my bumper sticker. I told him I hadn't got around to it yet.

Excitement building about Together for the Kingdom. Have packed and unpacked at least three times. Vanessa called tonight and was positively bubbling over with ecstasy at the prospect of the conference.

"I just can't wait, Helen. I'm buying loads of extra food so that anyone in our group who wants to can stop by for a snack. One of the fabulous things about these events is that we don't have to all go home after a great evening, but we get to hang out and spend some quality time. In our church back in the States, we used to have loads of fellowship meals. I loved them."

There she goes again — slightly odd, beautiful, caring Vanessa.

Dad called and asked if I was okay and managed to perform a parental miracle: he said that he missed me, without giving the slightest hint of feeling that I have been neglecting him and Mum a bit lately, which I have. Somehow the tone of his voice and the words he uses convey absolute concern and love, without any strings attached or demands. He really is the best.

Friday, April 22

At Together for the Kingdom

Traffic jams tend to make an atheist out of me. I want to be able to speak at great big trucks and command them,

"Be thou removed and cast into the depths of the sea," but it doesn't ever work. And although I've been so looking forward to going to this event, the crawling traffic meant that I did a lot of thinking today and that made me feel worse. I'm now almost certain that whoever is speaking at the opening celebration will stop suddenly in the middle of the sermon, point straight at me, speak my full name ever so slowly and loudly, and announce to the crowd that a loose woman (or at least one who was seriously tempted to be loose, until a committed pagan gentleman rescued her from herself) is in their midst. The drummer will do a melodramatic roll, which will then turn into the kind of beat they play before the murderer is executed, a spotlight will slam blinding light straight into my eyes, and the stewards will hand out stones to everyone in order to facilitate the public execution. I will die, sobbing and bloody and sorry, but with no opportunity to offer tearful, repentant last words. I will breathe my last, the stewards will remove my limp yet still warm body from the service, and then they'll invite the band to come back, do another song, and take the offering.

Obviously, it's when I'm driving that I daydream the most and that dark little fantasy was giving me a cold sweat, but the fact is that I do feel so guilty again. But I've noticed that my guilt is selective, which is odd. I do feel really bad—not so much about what happened with Aaron and what I wanted to happen, but what I'm sure would have happened if Aaron hadn't refused to take advantage of me. I realized too that, although I thought that Aaron could be a bad influence on me, the truth is that on that sofa in the bookshop I was potentially the bad influence on him.

Now am feeling guilty because I have a confused capacity for guilt. This is getting worse. I do hope that I have a cataclysmic encounter with God this week that somehow will sort out all this mess and not involve me being pummeled with stones.

At last I saw the huge resort complex where the event is being held, so I parked my car, found a cart, and went looking for my cabin, which is always an agony for two reasons. First, I was loaded up like a pack mule with three plastic carrier bags cutting into my fingers like cheese wire. But the other pain was seeing all these other Christians arriving and unloading. Just looking at them makes me suspect that they don't have the same worries and sins and fears and, unlike me, they don't have to worry about James being in love with me, and my odd Mum sometimes, and lovely, eccentric Vanessa, and Aaron with the gin, and Kristian with the lovely grin, and Hayley the poor, sad, vicious, wounded little cow, and Mr. and Mrs. Hemming ... All the other arriving pilgrims at Together for the Kingdom look confident, happy, and connected to God with spiritual broadband. They probably sang hymns in the car on the way here today. They know where they're going in life. I can't even find the right block of cabins because I'm tired and the idiot who created the big map of the site cunningly hid the section where my cabin is out of sight.

Dear God, here I am. Helen. Sloane. It's me and just as I've staggered across the site today with my bags and gro-

ceries and extra chocolate cookies and those plastic shopping bags from hell, so I come to you with all my stuff.

Jesus, you say your burden is easy. Mine isn't. Can we
do a swap?

Have to get ready to go to the opening service. Hoping
no stones being prepared.

Midnight

I survived the opening celebration service without becoming a victim of capital punishment. James is working a
late-evening venue on the sound desk, and Vanessa has
gone off to the 24/7 prayer tent with her laminated map, so
I decided to have an early night. I am surprised to report
that, despite nodding off because of the long drive and
the less-than-riveting sermon from Romans chapter 4 (an
odd choice for an opening night), I did like this evening.
I decided to tell God that I would worship him, but that I
had nothing to say. I'm too tired and a bit too confused to
string a sentence together. So I was so relieved when the
worship leader decided to lead us all in a beautiful piece
of liturgy. As the words came up on the screen, I realized that, when I don't have words, I can take the words
that have been written, perhaps hundreds of years ago, by
another fellow traveler, and I can make their words my
own. Feel strangely hopeful about this.

Jesus. Don't know what to say, so I'll just say your
name. Over and over. Jesus. Jesus. Jesus.

Goodnight.

Question: If I decide to tell someone that I think they need to seriously reconsider their attitude toward something, does that make me as bad as Mrs. Hemming? Earlier on, Vanessa and I were in one of the cafés on the resort, and Kristian meandered over and plonked himself down and started going on and on about the young man who led worship for the Bible study this morning.

"What was the name of the guy who led worship today, Hel?"

Yikes. We're back to *Hel* again. I thought we'd got through that terrible phase.

"Not sure. I think his name was Jamie or something. Why?"

Kris wrinkled his nose.

"Frankly, I wasn't impressed at all, especially for an event of this size. I think the organizers could do a lot better."

Right. I think I have a vague suspicion about the identity of the "better" choice of worship leader. That would be Kris thinking that Kris is better.

Vanessa was absentmindedly flipping through her Bible as we nattered. I was delighted that she went on the defensive for Jamie.

"I liked it. I thought what he did was simple ... and good. He even took us through another piece of liturgy, which was very beautiful, and stopped the music whilst we were doing it so we could concentrate."

I chimed in. "I never realized liturgy could be so powerful. Must ask Robert and Nola if we can do a similar thing in our church."

Kristian wasn't persuaded. He said he wasn't too sure about the liturgy idea and wasn't the point of worship to sing? But he mentioned that he was sure that Jamie would want to meet him if he knew that someone with a similar anointing was also here. It was sad to see Kris being competitive, deriding a lot of Jamie's music. It was obvious —Kristian wanted to take his place. Eventually he started saying some really nasty things about the guy, which I found distasteful, and I said so and tried to change the conversation three times until he finally spotted someone he knew (I think that probably happens a lot to Kristian at Christian conferences), and he bounced off to embrace them in a big hug.

11:00 p.m.

If I knew Kristian was going to turn out to be such a creep, I wouldn't have bothered trying to tell him he shouldn't have been so horrible about that worship leader, Jamie. We were sitting in my cabin and Vanessa and James had gone out to get ice cream, and I was tentatively trying to bring up the conversation we had earlier. Which was ironic, as earlier on I couldn't get him to stop talking and now I couldn't get him to start. I thought that if I could get him to say something horrible again by bringing up the subject, I could use that as an example to demonstrate my point. Sneaky I know, but God did tell us to be as cunning as snakes ...

I managed to get around to the subject again by saying that I'd seen Jamie in the bookshop and had thanked him for his contribution.

"What did he say when you thanked him, Hel?"

"He smiled and said how much he appreciated my encouragement. Said he'd been quite nervous, and so he was glad I found the service helpful. I like him."

"I like him too, Hel, but I can't help worrying that this big platform opportunity has made him just a little arrogant. Maybe someone else, someone more humble, would be better suited to leading the worship in the main services. I have to say that I got the impression that Jamie was enjoying the whole performance thing too much; celebrity in Christian culture is completely against God's will."

By which point I got angry; I didn't think that Jamie was like that at all. If anything he seemed shy. So I started saying that I didn't think he should be so critical of him and that I'm sure he didn't ask to be treated like a celebrity, the way that some Christians treated him—and I was looking pointedly at Kristian as I said it, as I know he got Jamie to sign three CDs and his Bible yesterday . . .

Then suddenly, without word or warning, Kristian lunged toward my face and in a second started slobbering all over my mouth, pushed me back down on the couch, and tried a sneaky move with his hands.

I was in shock. I tried to move away, but he was pushing me down, so in the end there was nothing else for it: I had to knee him in the stomach. He's a worship leader, for goodness' sake, but I got the distinct impression that he had done this kind of thing before.

Anyway, I pushed him off, and in a firm, okay, admittedly shaky voice, I told him politely that it was definitely time to leave. And that if he ever tried anything like that again, I wouldn't hesitate about telling Robert and Nola.

Of course, he looked absolutely petrified. I wonder if a girl has ever refused him before ... He started apologizing, saying that he thought that was what I wanted ...

... and then he went into verbal attack mode. He said that by being alone in a cabin with him late at night, I had led him on and caused him to stumble. Can you believe that idiot? I was about to resort to the use of an emergency swear word when, thankfully, James and Vanessa appeared outside with ice cream.

Kristian is a phony. I was mad ever to like him. He may look cute, but what's behind the pretty-boy exterior is really ugly. He stormed off into the night, and I burst into tears and told Vanessa and James what had happened. They were aghast, and James looked like he was ready to kill. Vanessa calmed him down.

"But we can't just let him get away with that!" he yelled, when Vanessa suggested we pray about the situation.

"No one is getting away with anything," Vanessa insisted. "But we need wisdom to know what to do."

This much is certain: the blond, blue-eyed Abba children will never, ever materialize. At least one issue in my life is sorted once and for all. Kristian Vivian Rogers is history. So should I tell Robert and Nola about his unexpected and unwelcome moves?

Slightly weepy breakfast with Vanessa, who was very concerned that I not let last night rob me of the potential blessing that God has for me at this conference.

Perhaps emboldened by her encouragement, I went off to a seminar about doubt. The speaker did absolutely nothing for me whatsoever, and frankly I didn't understand most of what he was saying. To be honest, that might have more to do with me than his presentation. I can hardly think straight because I'm still so angry about last night. "I want to be a big Christian star" Kristian hasn't been seen by anyone today; it's like he's hiding away, probably worried sick about what I might say, especially if I decide to tell Robert and Nola. I was pondering all of this when I was suddenly distracted by one particular steward. I've been watching these stewards over the last couple of days and 99 percent of them are nothing short of wonderful. They work long hours, and the majority of them keep smiling and are patient and kind. Admittedly there is one large bearded bloke with a walkie-talkie who is obviously delighted to be in power. He's so gruff and rude that I think he'd be chucked out of the Gestapo for being too rough. He barked at me yesterday for leaving my Bible in the aisle. It was a health-and-safety hazard, he said, and didn't I know that someone could trip up over that Bible and seriously hurt themselves? Of course, he's right—it was a little careless of me—but he didn't need to bark at me like an Alsatian on speed and make me feel like the Witch of Endor just because I was a bit absentminded with my pocket-sized NIV. I apologized, but he muttered something and then started yelling into his walkie-talkie with a voice one would expect a Secret Service agent to use if the president had been shot.

The reason for his screaming was that the venue was running out of chairs. I noticed that when extra chairs were brought in, he did nothing to help the other stewards to put them out. He's loud, rude, and lazy with it. I'm trying to resist the temptation to use my "smite him with boils" prayer on him.

All of which makes the steward I was watching today even more wonderful. He is incredible. A couple of people came in late and wanted seats at the front, which were all taken. He had to tell them there was no room, and they started yelling about paying good money to come to this conference and you can't even get a seat. He flushed red with embarrassment but still held his cool and then went out of his way to find them two seats together nearer the back. They didn't even thank him. They were the last two seats available too. But then a man with a very large Bible and a huge notebook appeared—he looked like a very serious, scholarly type—and when that same steward had to kindly tell him that the venue was full and fire regulations meant that no one else could be accommodated, the serious notebook clutcher went off and started on about how he was going to complain because this seminar was on his specialist area of interest and it was so unfair that he couldn't get in and someone should plan these things more effectively and he was going to take this up with someone in authority.

The steward apologized.

It was then that the deep scholar sneered at him and said, "Your apology doesn't count. You're just a steward. I need to take this issue up with someone in authority."

And then the steward apologized yet again, whereupon the man stomped out of the tent. I was tempted to follow the rude angry idiot out of the tent and fell him to the ground with one expertly delivered judo kick (which probably wouldn't happen as my only initiation into the dark skills of martial arts was watching *The Karate Kid* when I was ten), but instead I realized that I needed to find the steward at the end of the seminar and apologize to him. I felt that the rudeness of these pompous idiots reflected on all the delegates at the conference.

Then I wondered if I was just expanding my seemingly never-ending capacity for guilt again. But at last when the speaker sat down and the seminar ended, I wandered over to the steward, who impossibly was still smiling and saying good-bye to delegates as they left the tent.

"I wanted to say how sorry I am about that man's rudeness to you and thank you for all your hard work," I stammered out, wondering if he would think that I was mad.

But the opposite happened. His smile got even bigger and we chatted for a while. I found out that sometimes he even comes to this conference as a speaker. His name is Jim and he's a consultant professor of business studies. He has a top job but loves to come and offer his time freely as a steward when he's not speaking. He's probably got a brain three times the size of the deep notebook clutcher. Most of his time is spent in the children's venues, he said. As a dad and grandfather, he loves to see the children learning about God. What a contrast to the "I want to be an international worship superstar" attitude of horrid Kristian.

I came away from the seminar a little exhausted from all my internal wrangling, but inspired and encouraged by watching Jim and chatting with him for a while. Some people can't help being a blessing.

Monday, April 25

8:00 a.m.

Got up super extra early to pray, go running, and generally be holy. That incident with Kristian has made me feel terrible. I feel like I've done something wrong, even though I'm sure I haven't. I keep running the incident through in my mind. Maybe I've misjudged the situation and it wasn't as bad as it seemed. I feel that if I was a better person, this wouldn't have happened to me.

Lord, please take this feeling away. Perhaps kissing Aaron put some sort of horrible thing in my life and Kristian was picking up on that. Lord, I know I've already asked you this, but please forgive me.

6:00 p.m.

I am writing this in a café, trying not to let my tears drip on the keyboard, but I'm okay. I've had an emotional afternoon and in some ways the outcome is depressing, but I have also managed to resolve a few important issues. I now feel like an independent woman who has a firm grip on her life. Okay, it's more like a loose finger grip on a greased pole, but nonetheless it is the beginning of a grip.

James turned up at my cabin this afternoon and, after shuffling around at the door for a bit, finally asked if I would like to go for coffee. Of course, when he said "coffee," he might as well have said marriage, children, and matching coffins. Why is asking someone for coffee in Christian circles such a big deal? I wondered whether, if I decided to go, I was somehow committing myself to a lifelong relationship of sound desk support and folding James's underwear?

Anyway, I decided that this thought was far too neurotic and told James that although I didn't fancy a coffee, I wouldn't mind another one of those vanilla and chocolate milkshakes that I succumbed to yesterday.

On the way there, we bumped into Vanessa, who gave us a lovely smile and hurried off to what was probably her eleventh seminar, workshop, or preach that day. We sat down. James bought the milkshake. I panicked. Does letting James buy me a milkshake mean that we are now in a committed relationship leading to marriage?

I decided for a moment that James was lovely and wondered what it would be like to kiss him, but then my mind rebelled and I found myself imagining kissing Aaron instead. Hormones sometimes have no discipline. Anyway, while I was imagining kissing Aaron, (well, not imagining, more replaying), I suddenly realized that James was looking at me like he expected an answer to an important question. I am a terrible person, sitting across the table with what could be my future husband, imagining kissing some agnostic bookshop worker who has, I suspect, a burgeoning drink problem.

"Sorry, I wandered off there. What was the last bit?" I asked him. He looked instantly dismayed.

"The thing is, Helen, you see, I don't want to put, um, any sort of pressure on you, and if you would prefer not to talk about this today, then, um, I guess that's fine. Because I know you might be confused at the moment because of some people." (With this he clenched his jaw.) "But, you see, I was wondering whether you could tell me whether you have been thinking that anything would ever, um, happen between us, because I've kind of noticed some tension in our friendship. Have you been hoping for something more?"

I looked into his face, and it was the face of lovely James who, yes, would make a great husband and a fantastic father. James, a good man and a man who loves God. And suddenly I had this realization, something dawned, and I looked at James in an entirely new light.

You see, I have had a revelation. The reason I had never resolved my feeling for James is because I never believed that God had anyone else out there for me. I thought that James was my one chance, and that the reason why I wasn't attracted to him was because there was something wrong with me. But there is no spiritual reason why I don't fancy James; I don't fancy James because, well, I don't fancy James. It doesn't mean there's anything wrong with him or that there's anything wrong with me either. It is how it is.

This took me some time to realize, and by then James looked like he was either going to burst into tears or was passing something particularly tricky through his lower intestine. So at last I spoke.

"James, I think you're a lovely man. I think you're kind and loyal and godly. But I don't think that we were meant for each other. Have you been hoping for something more? If so, I'm very sorry."

James looked a little bit too relieved for my liking. "Oh no. Not at all. I mean ... don't misunderstand me, Helen, I think you're lovely. And I love being your friend. But to be honest, I don't think about you like that at all ..."

I didn't know whether to be relieved or offended. I decided to opt for the former. But James was looking worried.

"Helen, if you don't mind me asking—you haven't got your sights on Kris, have you? Because, Helen, I'm saying this because I'm your friend. I don't think I trust him. In fact I don't trust him at all."

"I know," I replied. "Don't worry, I am never going to go near Kristian Rogers again."

James looked relieved. And suddenly jumped up. "Listen, Helen, I'd better go, because there's a seminar I said I'd go to with Vanessa. No hard feelings, yeah? I hope we can still be friends without feeling awkward around one another."

"Sure." I smiled and kissed him on the cheek. "No problem."

He left. I thought that if that man doesn't believe things are going to be awkward, then he has the emotional intelligence of a wombat. Things were going to be as awkward as King Herod being the Director of the Bethlehem Playgroup Society.

And then the strangest thing happened. I started to cry. Though I felt better for having resolved this situation with James, I felt a little lost. I have one horrible man who likes me a little too much for comfort (or at least tried to like me a little too much for comfort), I have one lovely man who just wants to be my best friend, which makes me 98 percent glad and 2 percent sad, and I have one super sexy guy, and I don't want to date him because he isn't a Christian. I am officially a failure with men.

I looked around the coffee shop, and all I seemed to see were wedding rings. I mean, people fall in love all the time. How hard can it be?

Then suddenly a smiling woman came up to my table, wearing a steward's coat and a big badge on her lapel that says Counselor. Uh-oh, I immediately thought, because I've always thought it was a bit strange that Christians seem so eager to tell their deepest, darkest secrets to people they don't even know. She asked me if I was all right, and I tried to hold back the tears and say that I was fine. But it came out in a bit of a wail, and I ended up telling her about everything — about Kristian and James and Aaron. About how I didn't know if I believed that God had a husband for me and that no man would ever love me anyway because I am clearly a Jezebel and am not the kind of girl who would ever be allowed to sing in the backing group for a worship leader …

"It seems to me," she said after I had finally stopped hiccupping in her lap, "that just because you got very close to doing something you'd regret doesn't mean that you're broadcasting that fact to every man in the universe. And secondly, if you're not that great, then why does an amazing man like James seem to like you so much, even if it is just as a friend? Helen, maybe your problem is that you spend far too much time arguing with God."

She prayed for me and offered to spend more time with me, but I said it was okay. To be honest, I was annoyed at this point because I don't think that I argue with God. I'm always asking him to tell me what to do and trying to obey him. I may get things wrong sometimes, but I never argue! This is why it's such a bad idea to pour your heart out to some stranger, who probably got married when they were nineteen anyway and who has no idea what it's like to be twenty-seven and single.

But strangely, I still do feel a little better about everything now.

Lord, please keep working in my life. Sort out my head. And my heart. Amen.

At Bedtime

Slightly iffy news: still no sign of Kristian. I am slightly worried, but I think he's lying low to give it a day or so for things to blow over. Bad news (I think): James seems too relieved by my telling him that nothing's going to happen between us. It's funny, really, because that's exactly what I want, it's even what I've prayed for—but it would be helpful if he'd appear ever so slightly disappointed ... Good news: I think that I've actually made a serious step forward tonight in my "I'm a wicked witch and I'm broadcasting lust vibes to every man on earth" hang-up. Despite all the criticisms of these mega-Christian events, I actually think that I've met God today and that a lot of things are falling into place.

I became increasingly angry after that counselor woman told me I argued with God. What a nerve. I went back to my cabin and read the story of Jacob wrestling with God. It took a long time, because of my using the Amplified Version that I borrowed from Vanessa ("Jacob wrestled, fought, struggled with, contested with God, the Lord, Yahweh, Jehovah"). Okay, I get the point. But I don't get the point of that counselor's comment. I do make loads of mistakes, but this wrestling idea seems to mean that I am fighting what God wants to do in my life. Half my angst is the fact that I do want God's will for me. In fact, sometimes I envy Laura's uncomplicated way of living. She doesn't worry about eternity, God's will, the world, angels, demons, and a host of other things that fill my head—she gets on with living.

Anyway, I spent some time telling God that I don't think that I argue with him but I am willing to be shown that I argue with him if I do because I don't want to argue with him about arguing with him ...

Felt more confused than ever, and so I was not looking forward to the service tonight. I mumbled my way through the worship, took exception to the song choice, wrote the woman off who was going to preach as a token Christian woman leader ... and then realized that with an attitude like that no one can win—when there's not a woman up there, we get mad and when there is, we write her off as token. I realized that sometimes people get upset with things that happen in churches and conferences, but the issues that they complain about are not the real issues at all. They're not happy and are finding ways to express their unhappiness—anything will do.

I'd pretty much written off the evening as worthless when the lady who was preaching started into her talk. She took me off my guard because she was warm, funny, and very vulnerable. She opened up the sermon by telling us about some ridiculous things that she'd done—and some mistakes that she'd made. I immediately liked her because here was someone who is obviously passionate about God and heading in the right direction, but who wasn't afraid to admit that she trips up too.

And then she got down to the business of opening up the Scripture text, which was that bit about Peter having a dream where God lowers a sheet full of non-kosher animals and commands highly Jewish Peter to snack from it. The preacher lady said that as Peter was a good kosher boy, this was the cultural equivalent of God lowering a fully stocked bar into a Salvation Army service on a Sunday morning and saying, "The drinks are on me, ladies and gentlemen"—and so understandably Peter refused. And then God said to Peter, "Don't call unclean what I've called clean"—and so Peter did as he was told.

The preacher lady told the story hilariously, and I roared at the way she described the scene — and then suddenly, even as I was laughing, something hit me like a ton of bricks. Peter was arguing with God as he insisted on tagging something as unclean — and that's exactly and precisely what I've been doing with myself. God says that I'm clean, and yet I struggle with the idea, think I'm doing God a favor when I beat myself up, and even treat forgiveness like a dieter would treat Belgian chocolate — a rather indulgent luxury that I don't deserve, would like to enjoy, but should probably refrain from. I'm like some ancient monk whipping myself and drawing blood and thinking that he's pleasing God as he rips off a bit more flesh — or even a bit like old Simeon up the pole who thought that God was pleased with him for parking in his own filth for years.

If God's final and unalterable verdict about me is that I'm clean through what Jesus has done, then who am I to disagree? Arguing with God is not just about wicked rebellion and refusal to do his will — it's also about refusing to accept his blessings and gifts of love.

Anyway, at the end of the sermon the preacher lady brought out a huge, beautifully packaged gift tied with rich gold ribbon — and talked about how sad a father would be if he'd sacrificed hugely to make sure that his son or daughter could enjoy a gift — but they refused to even open or accept it. We needed to repent of our guilty arguing, she said.

I cried buckets — for the second time today — and went forward for prayer at the end because it was obvious that

God was talking to me. I felt bad about my judging the counselor lady too; obviously she planted a seed in my mind and somehow God pulled it all together. When I went forward, James came out too and stood with me while I prayed, which I thought was nice.

I got together with Vanessa in the cabin afterward, and she obviously wanted to tell me about all the seminars she had attended and the "alternative" worship service tonight, which involved people painting their emotions on a huge easel. But she listened quietly as I told her everything: James, Aaron, the whole sorry mess, but I also explained what had happened today with the counselor and then the sermon tonight. She was lovely. And unexpectedly clear in her response. She read me the story from the Bible about Peter refusing to allow Jesus to wash his feet—another argument with Jesus, she said, and about how Jesus had absolutely insisted that Peter let him do that.

"Jesus warned Peter that, unless he allowed the foot-washing thing, he could have no part with him. Think about that, Helen ..." She paused and eyed me. "The only way we can be with Jesus is on the basis of this marvelous arrangement—we allow him to clean us up. Unless we do, this Christian thing won't work."

I cried again and it was all rather wonderful until I suddenly noticed that Vanessa was kneeling down in front of me and tugging at my feet. She'd grabbed a washing-up bowl from the sink and filled it with warm water, added some salt for some symbolic purpose, and was now proposing to wash my feet as a reminder of this day. I didn't want it to happen, not least because I was wearing tights, which means that (a) I'd have to take them off, which would be a bit weird or (b) end up with soggy tights, which would be worse.

I tried to explain and beg off. Vanessa was frustrated, to say the least, having envisioned a very charismatic and representative moment.

"You're acting just like Peter!"

"Vee, Peter was very probably not wearing tights."

Although still disappointed, she eventually seemed okay about my not wanting to do the foot-washing thing.

The great thing is that I think I'm starting to realize that forgiveness is not about feelings, about taking advantage of God, or about being a wimpy Christian—grace and forgiveness sit at the heart of everything. When you know that you've been forgiven, then you'll go all the way with God, like Peter did. Maybe he remembered the foot-washing incident after he denied Jesus, and the memory of it helped him to finally find peace about his betrayal ...

I am exhausted from all this emotion and thinking. Good night.

Tuesday, April 26

10:00 a.m.

The mystery of Kristian laying low is no mystery at all. It turns out he's been hanging out with some other girl. They walked past me early this morning and she shot me a look as if I was the biggest weirdo since the Elephant Man. I dread to think what he told her about me — probably that I was completely obsessed about him or something. I've been trying to decide whether or not to talk to Robert and Nola about what happened with Kristian. I know it's not a massively big deal, but I get the feeling that he might try the same thing with another girl in my church, who might not have the presence of mind to do anything about it. I think I'll go find Nola and see what she thinks about the whole situation.

1:00 p.m.

Have just talked to Nola and have also consumed a lunch that would comfortably feed a family of five. She says that she and Robert had already been keeping a close eye on Kristian and that they would pray about the situation. Robert had already had a quiet word with him about dating girls in the church and said that, as Kristian is a member of the pastoral team, he must talk it over with Robert before he decides to get "romantically involved" with anyone. I feel much better now someone has taken this situation out of my hands.

Thank you, Lord, for Nola and Robert, please give them the wisdom and strength to make the right decisions.

4:00 p.m.

I began the afternoon by going to a seminar on grief, which was awful. I'm not sure why I went really, but it said in the program that grief is one experience that every human being on Planet Earth will have to steer through, so I thought perhaps it would be good to be prepared. The man who led the seminar said that he understood grief because his cat had died recently, which was sad. But I felt terrible for the people sitting in the audience who were mourning the loss of their children or spouses; comparing their sadness to his seemed ridiculous.

Then he started talking about how he'd found comfort in the belief that his cat was now in heaven, which sounded nice and reasonable ... until I tried to imagine a ginger tabby in the sky with its paws raised singing "Blessed be the name of the Lord" along with the heavenly choir. And then I wondered if rats and lice got to go there too. And then I gave up, pretended that I had an urgent text message, left the seminar, and met Vanessa for coffee.

Now I have just returned from a songwriters' workshop. Yes. Me, whose untamed voice sounds like shrieking, attended a workshop about writing songs. I only went because Vanessa has decided that she would like to write worship songs. Apparently everybody wants to get in on the action. However, her efforts so far haven't been too bad — better than Kristian's anyway, which of course isn't hard. She managed to write the lyrics for a whole song yesterday without mentioning mountains, any type of body of water, or repeating the same phrase over and over again.

I am continuously struck by what an amazing woman Vanessa is. She is a bit loopy, but part of that seems to be the secret of her success as a human being. She doesn't seem to have the sort of problems I have, although sometimes I know she feels a bit overwhelmed. She talks a lot about the difference between the world as it is now and the Kingdom of God that Jesus spoke about all the time—and it upsets her. She says the amount of suffering in the world is absolutely sickening, especially since we seem to do so little about it. Sometimes she loses the hope that anything can be done at all and thinks that maybe the world should burn up in some kind of apocalyptic inferno. But when she feels that hopeless, she says she prays a lot more and that after a couple of days things feel better.

This songwriters' workshop put my mind at ease about Kristian. I'd been worrying about the part he plays in church life. I was nervous about what would happen if he did "make it" and people everywhere started buying and singing his songs. What would I have to do? Stand up at a huge worship conference and announce that he, in fact, didn't deserve to be there because of his false motives, judgmental attitude, and tendency to lunge at members of his congregation?

But who am I to decide who or who does not make it? And by that time he might have made some peace with God, or have completely changed, and I would be destroying his career.

All this has been niggling me. But now my mind has been put at ease.

The worship workshop was run by worship pundit Graham Kendrick, and Vanessa practically wet herself on the way. She went on and on about this song he wrote called "How Long?" which completely changed her life as a Christian. I've personally never heard of it, but I'm sure

Vanessa will play it to me, probably over and over again at some point, until I'm forced to ask the question "How long?" myself.

The workshop was split into two parts. In the beginning Graham talked about worship music, what made a good song, and about the kind of songs we should write as songwriters in order to serve the church. It was a good talk, and, strangely, he said everything I'd been thinking for so long in church about worship music! He stressed how we need to be more careful about what lyrics we put in our songs and that we need to be more like poets. He cited a few examples from some old hymns, and I suddenly realized how much theological and biblical knowledge those writers managed to cram into one line. He also mentioned that it would be fantastic to hear more songs that spoke about stories in the Bible, at which point Vanessa started bouncing up and down in her seat.

In the second half Graham invited people to share some of the songs they'd written, and we all discussed how we thought they could be better, in a very nice Christian way ...

Just before Kristian got up to share his song (which I noticed he seemed to have scribbled down during the talk), I noticed Graham leaning over and whispering something in his ear. Suddenly Kristian's face went bright red. Apparently (I heard afterward from James, there in his role of sound man, sitting next to Kristian) Kris had written a song about the biblical character of Ruth, but in his hurry he'd confused her name with Rahab, Boaz's morally negotiable grandmother. Graham stepped in at the last minute and saved Kris from totally embarrassing himself in front of everyone. Kristian didn't even look that grateful.

Then he sang his song, "I Am Ruth," during which he repeated the line, "Take me, take me, I breathe you, Lord," about twelve times, possibly more.

When Kris finally ended and looked around the workshop for an expected barrage of applause, there was embarrassed silence, which I think Kristian took as stunned awe, as he moved into his faraway eyes-half-closed and nodding routine and stood there at the mic going, "Yeah, Lord. Yeah, Jesus. Yeah. Mmm . . ."

It was at this point I realized that the Bride of Christ was safe from Kristian's minor-chord fumblings, at least for now. It didn't seem like he was going to go anywhere in worship music very fast, which, all in all, I thought was a very good thing. Finally, he sat down.

Vanessa was completely ecstatic because Graham said the song she wrote about King David was excellent and that though it might be better suited as more of a performance song, as he thought a congregation might find it hard to sing, he was sure that people would get a lot out of it. So it was an all-round good day for everyone, even Kristian (but in a way that he probably doesn't appreciate).

Thank you, Lord.

Oh, called home to Mum and Dad at lunchtime. My dad seems to be a bit down about this whole business with the council selling Lawrence House. But despite all that he still managed to encourage me, mainly by the way he listened to all my ramblings. He'd make a great counselor at one of these events. Whenever I'm upset he always says to me that our troubles can make us strong—if we go to God with them. I think he's right, although I would prefer strength and would like to pass on the troubles.

The rest of the day was uneventfully nice. I did have a bit of a minor crisis when I went to a seminar about calling and it seemed to be all about being church leaders or missionaries in some far-flung part of the globe, translating the Bible while existing on a diet of sheep entrails. Had a quirk of guilt again about leaving small-group leadership and focusing on the youth club (which opens this coming Friday—help!) but remembered Nola's advice about the Kingdom of God.

Wednesday, April 27

Drove home last night. This morning I experienced that rather strange deflated feeling that tends to land on me when I get to the end of a nice vacation or a Christian conference. Somehow everything seems slightly greyer when you get home and, of course, all the atmosphere of the big event is gone too. I've got a feeling that I've spent a long weekend in an unreal place and that there's no connection between the world that I've been in at the conference, and the "real" world that I've returned to, with out-of-date milk in the refrigerator and cat poop on my doorstep. But the more I thought about the counselor/arguing with God/Peter and hoofed animals/Vanessa and her good advice/

attempt to hold a ritual hosiery drenching, I decided that what I'd experienced was very real. Read and reread my journal and realized how good it was to have written it all down.

During the drive home, when the local young farmers seemed to have come out onto the roads for a tractor convention, I daydreamed unhelpfully about Aaron. All my holy dealings don't eradicate the moment of that rather terrific making-out session, but I decided that I am not going to contact Aaron for now. I wasn't good for him and he wasn't good for me either. And anyway, I've decided that if I am going to go somewhere in a relationship, I want it to be with someone who's full-on as a Christian. I've made that decision not simply because of something in the Bible about being unequally yoked. (To be honest, I'm not totally sure what that's about anyway.) It's that I do want someone who can understand this driving urgency that I've got to live for God. I love Laura, but actually I don't want her uncomplicated life: I don't want to live for nothing but the next day. I'm not judging her, but I know that I want more than that.

Back to work tomorrow. Looking forward to seeing Laura. Not looking forward to seeing Hayley. Just three days to the youth-club opening!

Back to earth with a bump. Mad day of catch-up at work. This morning I did my early morning run, and then as soon as I got in to the office, Laura took me to one side and said that there'd been a bad development in Hayley's case—it turns out that Hayley got into some serious self-harming while I was gone and ended up in ER. It definitely wasn't a suicide attempt, but she managed to cut herself badly enough to need medical attention.

This is new territory for Hayley—she's been an abuser of other people so effectively that she could probably get an honorary doctorate in cursing, but this is the first time, to my knowledge, she's actually turned on herself. To make things worse, apparently she called the office to speak to me while I was away yesterday, but when the duty social worker said I'd be back in today, she gave them another epic mouthful and slammed the phone down. Very early this morning, her aunt left a message on the office answering machine to say that Hayley had been an outpatient last night, that she'd been fixed up and was back home now, and that none of this would have happened if we duffel-coated stuck-ups in Children's Services were around to do our jobs. Apparently Hayley had gone back to the bloke in the caravan park and had found him with someone else, which threw her into a mad session with a sharp knife. She's going to be okay, but the scars will be nasty.

Went straight round to her house—but she was out with her friends, and so I got yet another tongue-lashing from her dysfunctional guardian. The conference seems like ancient history now. I'm going to reread my journal again now to remind myself of what happened.

Friday, April 29

Well, it was a small start, but we've begun. The council wouldn't let us take down all the old photographs of long dead councilors that line the walls, so there's a feeling that there are old people glaring at us all the time—but it's okay. We got a great foosball table, which we bought from the little offering that the small group took on my leaving night. The place feels like a classroom, which of course isn't likely to create a line of kids at the door. But we have to start somewhere. Only seven kids showed up at first, including one of the gals who hangs around a lot with Hayley and who said that Hayley had a message for me.

"She wanted me to tell you, what was it she said—oh, yeah, she wanted you to know she wouldn't be seen dead in your pathetic little club."

That girl is one hurt piranha.

I started to get a little bit upset but then got a grip and decided that nothing was going to ruin the first night. A little bit of stress crept into the evening when another three kids showed up and said that they weren't going to wait their turn for the bleeping pool table because they bleeping well wanted to bleeping play now and if they bleeping well couldn't, well, then they'd tell all their bleeping friends what a complete bleeping waste of space this bleeping bleeping bleeping bleeping youth bleeping club was.

I was still smarting from Hayley's nastiness, so I was ready to kick them out on the spot, but James's computers saved the day. He invited them to save Planet Earth from an intergalactic monster that was running riot through the subterranean caverns of an underground kingdom by nuking it with a laser. This they did happily and even ended up watching another couple of kids play pool and then took their turn with a compliance that was surely a miracle — almost as epic as the raising of Lazarus, although not nearly so smelly.

At the end of the evening, James helped tidy up and then lugged all his computer equipment into the car — he worked hard.

I thanked him for praying for me and for doing the offering at the small group, which meant that we had a foosball table, and then coming and helping out at the club. And then I gave him a nice warm and appropriately brief hug of thanks, with three swift pats on the back, and drove home. James is a good man.

Sunday, May 1

In church this morning we had one of those "Let's share what God did for us while we were away at the conference" times, which I'm never sure is a good idea because it can send a message to those who didn't go that God's presence was tangible at Together for the Kingdom but they missed it. But we, the elite, who were there, now glow in the dark and are streets ahead in faith from the poor, empty souls who didn't go.

Kristian shared about how he met the Lord at the conference, which almost prompted me to choke, because he almost met my fist that night in the cabin. He also said that God had given him a song at the conference and that it had made a tremendous impact on everyone. So untrue, unless you count those healed of insomnia while he was singing it.

Robert spoke on praying for those who need the Lord, and I suddenly realized that I had spent more time kissing Aaron than praying for him.

Lunch at Mum and Dad's was a bit traumatic. Lovely to see them again, but Dad was quiet during the meal. Afterward Mum got on the phone to book a slot with her yoga teacher, and so Dad and I went for a walk and he got up on his soapbox.

"There's a big meeting at the Town Hall on Saturday about Lawrence House. Hopefully it will be an opportunity for the community to unite against such blatant corruption, a chance to reclaim something that belonged to them in the first place." Dad shook his head. "Do you know the council even tried to keep quiet the fact that we're having the meeting, so not many people would come?"

"Wow, very uncool, Dad."

"Well, your mum and I are trying to pack out the hall. There's a chance that if enough people know what the council's planning to do, we can shame them into changing their minds."

"Okay, then I'll come too and try to get as many of my friends to come as possible."

"Thank you, darling." He gave me a hug.

I'd do anything to take the worn look off his face.

When I got back to the flat tonight I called Vanessa, who called James, who called Robert and Nola, who called most of the church. Nola called me just now and said this is exactly the kind of thing the local church should be involved in and it is important that the community keep this building.

In a fit of madness, I even invited Laura from work, who surprisingly said she'd come. Dave has finally left her. I think she must be feeling a bit lonely.

Also texted Vanessa to say that I want us to get together for lunch tomorrow to talk about praying for people we like or love who don't know God. Like Aaron. And Laura.

Wednesday, May 4

Vanessa and I have called the prayer meeting. James is coming too. I am actually getting into prayer at the moment. All this running means I have been praying loads, partly for something to do, partly so God can send an army of angels to carry me up the next hill and perhaps provide a water fountain. But mainly to talk to God. The funny thing about praying is that once you start, sometimes it can be difficult to stop. I have been praying so much more the last few days that sometimes I don't even seem to notice I'm doing it. Sometimes I'm not even talking out loud or in my head, I'm kind of generally including God in what I'm doing. I find myself saying, "Look at that tree. Isn't it beautiful?" or "That woman looks sad; please comfort her."

Anyway, I've been praying for Laura and Aaron a lot, and after Robert's talk on Sunday I felt the need to get together with some other Christians to pray for them some more.

Lord, please give us the right words to say. Please let Aaron and Laura see what I see in you.

Thursday, May 5

I've been reading Psalm 4, which says that some people love delusions. Thinking about Aaron's bookstore today, wondered if that verse applies to some of the stuff in there. Do people love complex, almost illogical ideas because they're not really looking for answers—they just get a kick out of asking questions? Then I thought that there's also a very powerful place for questions—one that the church needs to reclaim. Questions can be holy, even when they don't lead us to answers.

Well! What I thought would be a relatively straightforward prayer meeting in Vanessa's family room ended up with me lurking in an alley outside Aaron's bookshop and hiding behind a bush in Laura's front yard. It all started off pretty normal. Vanessa had baked cheese straws in the shape of little crosses and James had brought along a bottle of grape juice. We had been praying for about forty minutes, and I must admit I was getting into it.

So we were praying when suddenly Vanessa had this idea.

"Okay, we should go and pray over the places where Aaron and Laura spend a lot of time."

We looked at her. "Huh?" I said.

She shrugged. "It's important to not only pray over a person but also the place they inhabit, so we should go to both of their houses and reclaim the ground for God."

Normally I would be against such ludicrous ideas, but for some reason I agreed to go along with this one.

"Right, then. Let's get a move on." James started packing the cheese straws into his pockets for provisions and even produced a Starbucks thermos from somewhere to keep the grape juice in. That man thinks of everything.

So we were prepared as we proceeded to "Go forth and conquer the powers of wickedness!" as Vanessa put it.

First we went to Laura's house, as I have no idea where Aaron lives. We could see her inside through a crack in the drapes. Vanessa wanted to march round the house seven times like Joshua did in the Bible, but James and I managed to dissuade her by saying the walls might fall down and we were trying to bless Laura, not destroy her home. Luckily, Vanessa had come as prepared as Buffy the Vampire Slayer in a graveyard. She had holy oil from

Israel, a flask of communion wine, several ornate crosses, and a stick of incense.

"Go hide behind that bush and start praying," she told me and James. I'm sure I saw a glimmer of a smirk on her face when she said it. "I'll go and consecrate the ground with the communion wine and oil."

By that point I had given up protesting, as Vanessa was clearly a woman with a mission. So I let her get on with it whilst I halfheartedly prayed for Laura's revelation that Christ was in fact the one true King of the Universe. James said we should hold hands, as it would unite our spirits against the darkness and make us more powerful warriors of Christ. I decided that he and Vanessa had definitely more in common than I had previously thought.

Vanessa took ages and by the time she came back, my hand was definitely feeling sweaty, and we had both run out of things to pray, so we were generally standing in the bushes, holding hands and feeling a bit awkward. At least I was feeling awkward. I kept on wanting to let go of his hand, but then I thought it might offend him so I didn't. I then wondered if he was thinking the same thing and worried that, in fact, he didn't want to hold my hand either, despite being the one to suggest it, and had started to panic. Luckily Vanessa came back just in time, as I was trying to decide whether to kiss James to see what would happen or let go of his hand and run away.

Because we didn't know where Aaron lived, we decided to go to the bookstore where he worked. So we made our way to Penny Alley. We all stood outside the store for a bit, and I think we both felt a bit stupid. By now, even James, who I've never heard say a bad word about anyone (except perhaps Kristian) was looking a bit fed up.

Then I noticed a little alley by the side of the shop and decided to investigate.

I made my way carefully down the shadowy lane, almost breaking my neck on a few boxes, when I noticed that light was spilling out of a little window. I took a quick look and realized Aaron was asleep on the old battered sofa in the back of the shop. I remember that sofa well. His chestnut curls were all mussed up on the arm of the sofa, and he had an almost empty bottle of gin falling out of his left hand onto the floor. His shirt was off, and I suddenly had a huge rush of feeling for him. I wanted to hug him and never let go. I thought maybe I could help him get over whatever it was he was going through.

I also noticed there was a smoldering cigarette in the ashtray and started desperately praying that the bookshop wouldn't burn down. I so wanted him to be safe.

As I stumbled back up the alley, I bumped straight into James. Vanessa was standing there too, having anointed all four corners of the store doorway with oil.

"He's in there. He's asleep—but I'm worried there might be a fire." James went and took a look through the window and came back in a few seconds.

"It's all right, Helen. He's still asleep, snoring his head off, but the cigarette has burned out. He's fine."

And at that Vanessa announced that we should go as we'd done what we'd come to do, and we went home.

Lord, please watch over Aaron for me. Be there as he sleeps. Amen.

Today I finally got to see Hayley—but I couldn't get much out of her. She just said she hated men but she hated me more. I invited Hayley to come along to the youth club tonight. She invited me to go to hell and told me that she'd rather have her head amputated.

Progress is somewhat limited with Hayley. She's still angry about last Christmas. One of the most difficult things that I have to deal with is doing difficult things to protect people who don't understand what I'm doing and who therefore resent my care. They hate me because they think I'm trying to mess up their lives when, in fact, I'm trying to do the opposite. Hayley's one case in point, but I have others. I'm trying to protect these kids from parents who are inadequate, in some cases predatory, or too out of it to care, and yet some children seem unable to get to the point where they acknowledge that their parents can do anything wrong. In fact, they'd rather blame themselves than admit to the fact that their dad is bad.

Then I wondered if perhaps that happens to God all the time. There are some things that he definitely says no to that are off-limits for Christians. But that's not because God is a cosmic killjoy who is spending eternity trying to louse up our fun, but because he knows what damage we do to ourselves when we mess around with stuff that will hurt us. He wants to save us from pain. What kind of parent would allow their child to put their hand on a hot range or in a fire or play with rattlesnakes? Good parents say no. But just as kids think that their parents are sad and don't know anything, so perhaps we do the same with God. Next time I feel resentful because as a Christian I'm not free to do whatever I want, I need to remember that the God who says no does so because he is love.

Of course, that's not so easy to remember when the pressure is on ... but Lord, remind me.

I'm still praying lots for Laura and Aaron. Laura is one of the funniest women I have ever met. I sort of feel bad for laughing because some of her humor is not the most complimentary to people, but she makes these hilarious gags while at the same time keeping her face totally straight. Sometimes I'm not even sure whether she means to be funny or not. Today she was doing an impression of Hayley, who came screaming into the office to demand some more money. Every time she asked Laura a question, Laura replied in exactly the same voice and tone. Hayley couldn't figure out whether she was doing it on purpose or whether that was just the way she spoke. To be honest, I think she is frightened of Laura. She will swear at me, but she goes all quiet when Laura is around. I think she can sense that Laura won't take any of her nonsense. Plus, I'm not so sure I could take Hayley in a fight, despite being goodness knows how much older than her. Laura could restrain her with one hand. Sometimes I think that the only language Hayley understands is violence. At least it's the only language she's been taught.

Nola phoned me up today and you'll never guess who turned up at her philosophy class last night. Aaron! My stomach immediately did somersaults, imagining him converting dramatically as Nola proved with logic as sharp as Jack the Ripper's knife collection that God is indeed the true Master of the Universe and that Aaron's main purpose in life is to dedicate himself to Christ. Unfortunately, he seemed obstinate and kicked up a fuss about the impossibility of the Trinity. Which to be fair, I have never figured out either.

Nola had more news. "A few students and I went out afterward, and Aaron went too." She paused dramatically.

"And ...?"

"And he kept going on about this girl Helen whom he respects and who seems to get the Christian thing in a good way, despite, of course, her faith being horribly, logically flawed."

He was talking about me? I almost squealed.

"I asked him a couple of questions and finally figured out that it was you!"

I nodded happily, uncaring that she couldn't see me.

"See, Helen? I'm telling you this to encourage you. You keep going on about how you're not very good at the whole Christian thing, but here you just received some of the highest praise you can get. Helen, when someone who thinks that Jesus had some serious emotional issues and that Christianity is probably responsible for the death, torture, and rape of half the world's population believes you are a good Christian and a great person, it's time to realize you must be doing something right."

She seemed quite concerned for Aaron, though. She mentioned that at the pub he was drinking a lot and found it difficult to concentrate on the conversation. She said that as the night wore on, he got increasingly random, and she didn't think that drunkenness was the sole cause.

"Keep an eye on him, Helen."

Ironic, as I'm supposed to be keeping far, far away. I can't decide whether this is something Satan is doing to tempt me or something God is doing to look after Aaron, or even if life works like that in the first place. Maybe this is a completely random thing.

However, I'm sure that I couldn't handle the temptation of being alone with him again. Even if he sat very quietly in the next room, the sexual tension between us means we'd still be committing some sort of lusty act.

But Nola hadn't finished. "Something he said concerns me. He told me that at night he tries to sleep but he's terrified of what will happen if he closes his eyes. Sometimes he can't tell whether he's dreaming or awake, that there are times when he sees things outside his window."

I was instantly worried. Oh, Lord, this is worse than I thought.

Nola told me she'd invited Aaron to Dad's big meeting at the Town Hall tomorrow night and said he sounded enthusiastic about attending. I was glad, but nervous—I haven't seen him since that night at the café. I hope it's not horribly awkward.

Lord, please, please, please look after Aaron. I don't think I could bear it if anything bad happened to him. Please protect him and help him get a really good night's sleep.

Tonight, youth club was quiet but okay. One of the lads who comes seems to have some sort of Freudian nasal fixation. Honestly, it's like he's fishing for small change up there, or looking for his bicycle. And there's this other lad, John, who despite being clearly white and from Southern England insists on trying to speak like a black brother from the Bronx. Unfortunately he has a slightly posh mid-Sussex accent, and he keeps forgetting to be Bronx and reverts to upper-class twit mode, which makes the whole thing sound utterly preposterous.

Per example, a conversation tonight:

"Hi, John. How are you?"

"Hey, wassup, blud?"

"How was school today?"

"Alri't, innit? Me go lookin' for some hoes with me homies, miss, and then me went to me mates' crib, miss, and we smoke some ganja. Rather splendid ganja it was too, I must say."

"Lovely. How's your family?"

"Well, ma sista, she the hoe wot is biggin' it up riding the family horse in the show jumping today, and we is all hopin' she get de ribbon for first prize in the dressage. Thanks awfully for asking."

Of course, John's not crazy. He just hasn't figured out who he is or who he wants to be: a very common struggle among us human beings, whatever our age.

Lord, help John come to the realization that he is not a black rapper from New York. And help Dad tomorrow in the meeting. Let loads of people come. And may we win. Amen.

Finally, God, some real answers to all those prayers! We all bundled down to the Town Hall this afternoon for the meeting about Lawrence House. Even though we didn't have a vote, my dad said that there would be a good chance we could shame them into keeping the building, whether they liked it or not. It seemed like the whole town turned up, most of them enthusiastically shaking my dad's hand, saying things like "They won't defeat us again, you mark my words" or "This will be our revenge for the battle of the beach huts."

My mother was in her element. She was wearing an electric blue Jackie-O suit with an actual matching pillbox hat and red lipstick. She looked amazing, very sophisticated. I'd forgotten that my mother has the social networking ability of Bill Clinton on amphetamines — she had even drummed up the support of a few local celebrities. She was flitting from group to group, whispering, laughing, and shooting meaningful looks at the podium.

Outside the venue, I was shocked to see Aaron with some people I'm sure I recognized from the café we went to. At first I wasn't sure because they were all wearing red and had painted their hands and faces red as well. They were all wearing gags and blindfolds and were doing some sort of drama piece that basically involved them falling over each other. I recognized Aaron because he had written "rage against the machine" on the back of his T-shirt. Unfortunately one of the letters had faded so it read "Rag against the machine," which I don't think was his intended message.

I wanted to go and say hi but realized that with his blindfold and gag on, we weren't going to have a very productive conversation.

I found Laura standing, watching the red brigade with a bemused expression on her face. "Well, I never knew painting yourself red was the answer to the world's problems," she said wryly. "If everybody did it, perhaps all suffering and injustice would be instantly alleviated."

The bad news was that the infamous Councilor Pike was chairing the meeting. Apparently, he was the same guy who presided over the beach-hut affair and, at the meeting for that, had only asked the people who agreed with the project to speak. The rumor was that he had even paid some people in the audience to be on his and his cronies' side.

Anyway, eventually everybody filed in, and I noticed Robert and Nola in the crowd and realized that half of the members of our church were also there. I gave them a quick wave and sat down. Nola had explained to me the night before that Mr. and Mrs. Hemming would not be coming because they believed that if something was the will of God, it would happen, whether we did anything or not. And that if God wanted the community to keep Lawrence House, he would find a way for it to happen without our interference. Which didn't seem at all consistent with Mr. Hemming's frantic and brutal evangelistic techniques —which definitely constitute interference in my book . . .

Creepy Councilor Pike opened the meeting with a

greasy speech about the planned spa and waffled on about how it would only affect the community for the better, how there would be a swimming pool for the children to play in, and how in this current day and age, with society's problems with obesity and bad health, a spa was the best thing for this town to have. He went on to say that anyone who didn't agree with the sale of an otherwise empty building (that whilst standing disused was a drain on the council's resources) didn't want the best for this community and that the income from this proposed sale would go toward fighting street crime and building a new play-center for children. It all sounded very plausible.

However, halfway through his speech, my dad stood up. Gradually the entire room swiveled round to look at him. In the end, Councilor Pike stopped speaking and looked at Dad, his mouth open. I don't think I've ever seen my father look so angry; he's usually such a self-controlled man, but right then he was shaking with rage and even I found him intimidating.

He began, "I thank Councilor Pike for letting me speak. After the beach-hut debacle, I was beginning to think that freedom of speech had all but died in Frenton. I would like to make a few things clear. First, everything my colleague Councilor Pike has told you is a lie. This health spa will not be a place for the people of this community."

He raised his voice slightly.

"And the reason for that, as Councilor Pike knows only too well, is that eighty percent of the people in this community will not be able to afford to even walk through the front doors of this high-end luxury spa. Sure, children will be able to swim in the pool, as long as they are the children of the rich. This town will not be using this spa as a resource to get healthy, and part of the reason for that is that most of the good people of this town are too busy spending their money on extortionate tax bills. That would be the same tax that seems to be exclusively paying for the gas in your Porsche, Councilor Pike.

"And now, yes, this building is standing empty and it is currently a drain on the council's resources, so I suggest that we make better use of Lawrence House and turn it into something that the whole community can enjoy, both rich and poor alike."

With that he sat down and the whole place started clapping and cheering. Pike looked like he was going to explode, which would have been wonderful but messy.

And then Vanessa did perhaps the craziest thing I have ever seen her do. She ran up on stage clasping something fluffy and pink to her chest, launched herself on Councilor Pike, and before he could do anything to resist, had handcuffed herself to him and started yelling, "Free Lawrence House for the people" at the top of her voice. I think that everyone was supposed to join in with the chant, but everyone was too stunned to say anything.

Laura started giggling, and I suddenly realized that the handcuffs had "Lola's Erotic Emporium" written on them. Apparently James was in on the plot and they searched and searched for handcuffs, but the only place that sold them was Lola's, a dodgy-looking place on one of the little side roads off the High Street. James and Vanessa had decided to make a minor moral sacrifice for the greater moral good and went out to buy them. I must admit I'd pay a lot of money to have seen that little outing.

Anyway, by now Vanessa was looking slightly shocked at what she'd done. I think that in her head it probably seemed like a great idea, but the reality of having a disgruntled three-hundred-pound man latched onto your arm probably isn't that fun. He was trying to shake the cuff off, manhandling her in the process, and James was standing at the side of the stage shouting that he had better not hurt her. Laura was pretty much wetting herself at all this whilst a press photographer (my mother's idea) clicked away at the stage.

Councilor Pike was getting rough but there was no way out. Apparently James and Vanessa had symbolically thrown the key into the sea earlier that day, so there was no escaping the cuffs.

Suddenly Laura jumped up, mumbling something under her breath about how it's easier than you think to get out of those things, and she should know because that idiot Dave had been into them. Then she jumped on stage, did something complicated with a hair clip, and released Vanessa into James's waiting arms. This was a good idea, because I think if James hadn't been holding a shaken Vanessa, by the look on his face he would probably have been punching Councilor Pike hard by now.

Anyway, the synopsis of all this is that the meeting was such a success that the council surely can't possibly do anything but turn the building over to the community. Hurrah! Thank you, God. Well done, Dad. Even well done, Mistress Vanessa ...

Good but irritating church this morning. Robert gave an announcement thanking those who attended the meeting yesterday for their support and gave a brief report about what happened, although he didn't mention the handcuffing ... The irritating part came from one of the children. The Antichrist is alive and well and running round in his pants at New Wave church. He is only four and his name is Damien. To be fair, the Morrisons did think they were naming him after Saint Damien, the patron saint of leprosy, probably in a bid to cure Mr. Morrison's flaky skin, which has been known to bury small children, or at least create landslides.

Anyhow, after the church service I was attempting to thank Robert for his support yesterday when Damien Morrison, son of Satan, Antichrist on high, ran toward me, sticky fingers clenched, mouth (dripping abyss to hell) screaming, fat arms pumping, begging to be picked up. Some other children had been chasing him—probably the prophetic ones, hopefully with swords of fire—and I was obviously the first fool in his sight line who could provide him with some limited safety. I picked him up and held him for a few seconds, and he expressed his gratitude by poking me in the left eye with a pudgy finger and smearing chocolate all over my new top that I had saved up for ages to buy.

Life's like that. Good stuff and irritating stuff all mingled together.

Vanessa invited me to go to Infusion tonight where they

have installed a smoke machine. I tell no lies. Halfway through the worship, which was led by a rock boy-band that couldn't stop jumping about and sprinkling their adolescent dandruff on everybody at the front, they turned the machine on. It was bizarre. They had already turned out the lights, and as I was being half blinded by the neon light show, I was also being half blinded by white smoke. This took my mind totally off God and instead made me stumble about and curse softly under my breath. Once I had regained my sight I looked around and saw that so many people seemed to either be in a state of complete ecstasy or crying their eyes out. I wondered whether the same thing would happen without the gimmicks, and, if it does, I think we should ask the very serious question: Why the gimmicks? I don't want to criticize a church that brings so many people to God every year, but it makes me feel a little uncomfortable. Why do we need all these things to worship? Jesus never had any of them, and he was the most perfect Worshiper of all time.

Am I turning into an Amish woman? Will I ultimately turn my back on all things modern and ride around Frenton in a horse and cart while dressed in a long Victorian gown? Who knows?

Wednesday, May 11

My father just called me crying. Crying. I have only seen my father cry once in my life.

Dad was crying because the council called an emergency meeting about crime at the same time the vote on Lawrence House was supposed to be going ahead. Crime is one of the priorities on my father's portfolio on the council, and if he hadn't attended the emergency meeting, they would have had good cause to fire him. Several other people, who would have voted against Councilor Pike and his elitist health spa crew, also had to attend. So, in the building committee meeting, the motion to sell Lawrence House passed by one vote.

I feel like nailing lumps of raw meat on these lowlife councilors and then setting them loose in a safari park filled with biologically mutated lions. Lord, it's not fair, why does greed always seem to win?

My dad then apologized for crying and said he was embarrassed to have dumped all his sadness on me, what with me having such a stressful job. And then he went quiet and said that there was something very important that he wanted me to know.

My dad has never left me in any doubt that he loves me; every time I see my parents I get a hug and kiss good-bye from them both and they never fail to say "I love you." But perhaps, when you say it a lot, there's a danger that it can lose its impact. Anyway, when Dad said that he wanted to tell me something important, I felt a flash of nervous panic—the crisis-driven nature of my job means that I tend to think that sudden and unexpected news is probably bad. Dad cleared his throat, coughed, and said, "Helen, I do love you very much. I wanted to make sure that you know it. You're a stunning person and a wonderful daughter. I'm so proud of you."

It was my turn to cry now.

We talked a little bit more about bad things making us strong if we go to God with them, and I gently reminded him that he's always taught me that, so now he needed to do the same thing, and I promised to pray loads for him. This battle might have been lost, I said, but the war wasn't over yet.

When I put the telephone down, I wished that I felt as confident as I had sounded.

Thursday, May 12

I called Vanessa today to say that we need some serious emergency prayer. I have a list as long as my to-do list at work. First off, I need to pray for Dad and his devastation about the council shenanigans.

Then we need to pray for my up-and-coming marathon. It's getting so close, and I'm scared I'll get an injury or pass out halfway through the race. My training has been going all right, though I must admit I have been missing out some days. Yesterday I was supposed to run ten miles, but I didn't get out at all—felt deflated and discouraged after Dad's news. I really want to complete this marathon, if for no other reason than the cash I can raise.

Must be more consistent with the training.

Then there's Aaron. I still can't get him out of my head.

I've actually called him a couple of times, but he's never in and doesn't own a cell phone, as he says they poison the soul.

My mother could also do with some prayer, as could Laura, Hayley, and the rest of her friends. Plus there're the kids who hang out at the youth club, which is ticking along all right ...

Anyway, I turned up at Vanessa's house and who should be sitting in the living room but Laura herself? Apparently, after the handcuff incident at the public meeting, Laura and Vanessa got talking and have even hung out a couple of times. Of course neither of them thought to mention it to me. Theirs must be the strangest friendship in the world—even weirder than Gandhi and Saddam Hussein swapping friendship bracelets.

Anyway, so we start praying, and Laura seemed relaxed with it all, though I could only see her out of the corner of my eye—which caused her to ask, a couple of minutes into it, whether I had a problem with my eye and did I want her to look at it? The thing is I was so embarrassed praying in front of her. It's not that I'm ashamed of my faith, but it was more the fact that I was ashamed of myself. I was scared of saying something that would give her a bad impression of what Christianity was like. Also, Laura sees me at work, warts and all, and I was scared she might think that all this very earnest and righteous praying was hypocritical.

Vanessa seemed pretty calm for once. She seems to have become more chilled out—with the obvious exception of the handcuff incident.

Anyway, by the end of the prayer time, it didn't seem that we had dragged Laura through an emotional tunnel of religious abuse, and she even said yes when Vanessa asked if we could pray for her. I nearly died. Vanessa put her hands on Laura's head and started praying a little too loudly, but apparently, now that they're friends, Vanessa does it a lot and Laura likes how it feels. Praise the Lord! Now I feel ashamed that I wasn't brave enough to ask Laura whether I could pray for her before. Sometimes the world needs people like Vanessa.

After the prayer, we chatted a bit and Laura mentioned that one of her favorite plants in her garden seemed to be dying, and whilst digging around she'd found the ground had been covered in some sort of oil. I suddenly remembered Vanessa's consecration of Laura's flower bed and stifled a giggle, though Vanessa as usual seemed impervious ...

Lord, thank you so much for today, prayer does seem to work. Make it work for Dad. Amen.

Thursday, May 26

It's been a whole two weeks and not much has happened, hence my lax journaling habits. No further developments on Lawrence House, although it doesn't seem like the sale to the spa company has gone through yet. Perhaps the nasty lawyers who work for the nasty councilors are doing their nasty paperwork behind the scenes.

Marathon training going well — been following my training schedule without a hitch. Great.

Bible reading not going so well.

Vanessa said the sweetest thing to me today. She burst through my front door and announced "Helen, I'm getting married."

This was news to me because I didn't even know Vanessa fancied anyone.

"Does he know about it?" I said, as a sort of joke.

"Nope," she replied. "He hasn't even asked me out yet, but I'm sure it's going to happen. I've been praying a lot about it, and I feel like it's the right thing."

"Well, who is it?" I pressed.

"James, of course. Who else?"

Before she said it, I never would have thought of those two together, but it makes perfect sense. He always seems to be a bit more animated around her, and she always seems to be a bit more stable when he's in tow. Vanessa wouldn't think he was boring because Vanessa doesn't find anything boring. It's all part of her personality — she thinks that everything is amazingly interesting, fascinating, and either sent by God or the devil to test, strengthen, or give us some sort of celestial message.

Lord, please let James fall desperately in love with Vanessa, and let them live their lives happily ever after. Please don't let either of them get hurt.

I haven't written in this journal for over a month—horrors! Lots of reasons: the pace of life, training, youth club, work, etc., etc., being the main ones … Marathon training well on track, but increasingly time-consuming.

Read Psalm 14, which says that to say there is no God is the work of the fool. Thought about Aaron and prayed that he would be delivered from his folly and then remembered that he had said that he still believed in God but just couldn't figure the whole Christian thing out. Haven't seen or heard from Aaron since the red brigade incident at the public meeting.

Vanessa has now declared her undying love for James, and apparently he's desperately in love with her too, which is helpful. He even produced a poem from his pocket that he had been working on all week to give to her, which Vanessa has learnt off by heart and stapled to her bra. Praise be to God. I can see another one of those quickie engagements coming that Christians like to pull off so much.

Of course, it does make me feel slightly bad that I'm still single. Okay, who am I kidding—it makes me feel like the spinster hag of lonely land. But I'm still happy for them. Praise the Lord indeed.

Yikes. Another two weeks of journal silence. Youth club fine, Hayley the same, Vanessa and James in bliss, Laura lunching with Vanessa weekly, church good, Hemmings quiet, running great. Silence from Aaron still.

I am now existing on a diet of chocolate-flavored whey and protein bars. I have decided that a French fry will never pass my lips again for the rest of my days.

I went to the gym today. Why is it that going to the gym is harder than working out? It's as if my body screams bloodcurdling protests at the thought of weight training.

Mrs. Hemming was there again in her gigantic passion-killer gym gear. Glad to see that she is doing her bit to prevent the males of the species drifting into wanton lust ...

I am desperately trying to prevent myself from becoming a health bore. Just a few months ago I was happily munching my way through a mountain of fat every day and my preference for a happy death would have involved drowning in a chocolate-filled trough. And yet now I find myself not only checking my calorie consumption and body-fat index, but I also have an urgent need to give everybody I meet an update of (a) how many pounds I have lost, (b) what my resting heart rate is, (c) how many miles I have run today, and (d) how many of my clothes I need to throw away because of my newly discovered svelte hourglass figure (I exaggerate slightly). Not only that, but I also want to snatch their burgers out of their hand. How swiftly the chomper becomes the self-righteous teacher of others ...

Sunday, August 21

Marathon Day!

And yet another month when my diary has been neglected. Why is it that I get one part of my life in order, only to discover that other areas go into havoc mode? Finished reading through the Psalms and am now into reading Nehemiah, which is nice and would be of special interest to those who work in the construction industry. After all of the disappointment with the loss of Lawrence House (still no developments yet, but the silence is ominous, and Dad doesn't mention it anymore), today has been like a rainbow that suddenly appears like magic after a downpour. After preparing for this day for months, I finally got to run the marathon. Call me an endorphin junkie if you like, but I am tapping this journal entry into my computer in the car on the way home. Good thing James is driving. This was a one-off, and I must record my elated feelings so that I can enjoy them again later and before I start to forget—again, the benefits of journaling. Need a clear mind to recount all the events of the day. Not easy with the computer balanced on my knees, but I'll do my best.

Woke up and bounced out of bed, eager to get on with the challenge ahead. The sun was shining for once, and I worried that it might be too hot to run in. Mum and Dad called last night to wish me well, which was lovely. I then began the day with a hearty breakfast of eggs, bacon, fried bread, and mushrooms—obviously absolutely nothing healthy about this whatsoever but decided that as I'm going to expend about a zillion calories by hurtling my body along a 26.2 mile course, then I need all of the proteins, fat, carbohydrates, and whatever else is secreted in a British fry-up.

I packed my sports bag, and then James and Vanessa came and picked me up. James said he wanted to be there to provide support, and Vanessa will be praying for me every step of the way, she says. Headed to the start but had to abandon the car eventually and walk. When we got there, I felt immediately intimidated with the same feeling that I got at the start of Together for the Kingdom. The place was teeming with marathoners. Admittedly, not all of them looked like accomplished athletes, and there were one or two who looked as if they wouldn't survive the first two hundred yards, but there were enough finely honed athletic types to make me feel like a Ford Focus driver at a Formula 1 race meeting.

The major blow of the day was that Kristian was also there — as a runner. He'd certainly kept that quiet. We haven't spoken much since the infamous incident in the cabin, but there he was, all irritating and stud-like in his big Australian shorts, more suitable for surfing than running but undeniably trendy, and wearing an oversized T-shirt with a graffiti design. He didn't even have proper running shoes but was obviously planning to make a fashion statement as he wore his Vans. He may walk with a limp for the rest of his life, but he'll look good as he staggers.

His beaming girlfriend was there too, obviously his appointed cheerleader for the day. She shot me another one of those "greetings, O freak" looks. I decided to smile and wave but confess that I was grinding my teeth together as I did it.

He smiled at me as if we were the best of friends. "Good luck, Hel," he said, giving me the impression that he thought that I was definitely going to need it.

What makes it even more irritating is that I actually saw him—there were so many people there that I am sure if I had wanted to spot him, I wouldn't have been able to.

I drenched myself in water and then the starter's gun went off. All the runners are given numbers that reflect how fast they think they are going to complete the course, which means all the really serious ones go off first, and the rest of us come along behind, in order of our capabili-ties—or inflated hopes, in Kristian's case. (He must have thought he was going to be as good as me, though as far as I know he has done absolutely no training—I've never seen him out running.) It means that you start the mara-thon walking because of the crush of people, and it was a good mile before the crowd had thinned out enough for me to be able to start actually running. I had visions of walking the whole course, which was daft . . .

The first couple of miles were very hard, simply because my brain kept telling me that I had so long to go. I've found that the brain is the biggest challenge with running. One training manual actually suggests trying to fool your brain when you get up in the morning by telling yourself that you're not going to run. You're supposed to change into your running gear, while all the while tell-ing yourself, "I'm not going to run today." You grab some coffee and then when your brain isn't noticing, you make a dash for the door and make a run for it—literally.

But about three miles in, I had a wonderful surprise —Laura appeared behind a crash barrier, screaming "Go, Helen! Go, Helen!" I had no idea she was coming. She even ran alongside me for a few yards, and I panted out how lovely it was of her to come.

"Nonsense," she said. "We all need someone to yell for us."

At mile 5 my brain was screaming at me to lie down on the pavement, order a pizza, and take a nap, so I practiced my little positive-thinking tricks to keep me going through to mile 6 and beyond. I thought of words like *power* and *glide* and *winner*. Not sure if this is slightly New Agey but it seems to work.

It was as I started on mile 7 that I got what I'm ashamed to say was a delicious surprise, one that I enjoyed far more than I should have.

I came around a long bend and saw Kristian at the side of the road, bent over and throwing up. His girlfriend was nowhere to be seen, still back near the starting line, but there were enough people in the crowd watching for this to be embarrassing for Kristian. He was now treating about four hundred people to a public display of vomiting —not exactly the profile and platform that he would have chosen.

I'd seen Kristian shoot off like a hare on fire as soon as the crush had thinned enough to let him, but now he was in a right state. He hobbled onto the pavement, lay down, and groaned—obviously those Vans had not served him well. Did I gloat? As if ...

Kristian even gasped out, "I think I might háve flu ..." as I cantered by. Oh puh—leez!

Thought about stopping, but he had the paramedic people with him and starting again is so hard ... and the temptation to have said something sarcastic might have proved too much for me.

As I jogged away, I suddenly realized why it is that I so dislike Kristian. He can't admit his weaknesses. He's out of the race not because of some mystery bug but because he probably didn't train, is arrogant enough to think he can do anything, and was more concerned about looking cool than wearing the right gear. But he can't face all of that, so he has to pretend that he's been mugged by a germ. Pathetic.

I carried on and then was totally stunned at mile 14 to hear Vanessa's voice booming at me. *"Come on, Helen Sloane! Victory's in sight. Don't back off now. You and God can do it!"*

Vanessa and James and Laura had met up (they were in on the secret of Laura's coming) and had walked to the 14 mile point—the course doubles back on itself so they had to go a much shorter distance than me!—and waited there for me. It's probably psychological, but it was as if fresh power surged into my legs as I heard them clapping and cheering.

Prayed for death at mile 21, which was where I hit the infamous wall. The wall is where you feel that you have absolutely no physical or emotional resources left—you want to give up. Carrying on was simply a matter of cold choice—no feelings, no emotions, nothing but "I'm going to do this." Managed to get through that terrible phase and at last saw the finish line in sight. Once again, I could hear Vanessa's voice bellowing out at me. She was actually yelling that bit from the Bible about running the race to win, at the top of her voice. Laura and James were clapping and cheering, and at last, feeling like a corpse, I crossed the line.

Which is when I experienced a resurrection of sorts. Suddenly, my near-dead body and dull mind seemed to register that I had done it—I'd finished the course, I'd raised the money, I was a marathoner. I allowed Laura and James to hug me, and Vanessa did one of her little charismatic dances, which no one seemed to notice. It was wonderful.

I must call Mum and Dad to tell them about my massive sporting breakthrough. And then I'm looking forward to a long hot bath.

Oh, my cell phone battery is gone, and the computer's going the same way ... will finish this diary later.

Tuesday, August 23

Nothing.

Wednesday, August 24

Nothing to say.

Thursday, August 25

Am cold. Shattered. Black-hole empty.

Monday, September 5

LOCAL COUNCILOR MURDERED:
Police Appeal for Witnesses

Well-known local figure Peter Sloan (67) was fatally stabbed last Saturday night in an incident that police describe as an act of "senseless, mindless brutality." The tragedy took place outside the Dog and Duck pub on Frenton High Street somewhere around 11:30 p.m. In a statement issued earlier today, a police spokesman said that passersby became alarmed when a large gang of youths, some of whom were obviously intoxicated, started goading a young man who was walking past the pub. The gang then attacked the young man, who is not able to be named for legal reasons.

Apparently Mr. Sloane was driving past and saw the fracas and stopped to intervene. Police say that witnesses' reports are somewhat scattered but that apparently the gang then turned on Mr. Sloane and kicked and punched him before delivering repeated stab wounds to his chest and arms. The police and ambulance services were dispatched, but Mr. Sloane died at the scene.

Mr. Sloane became a well-known figure in Frenton after his unsuccessful campaign against beach-hut developments last year. Insisting that the local council conduct themselves with greater openness and accountability, Mr. Sloane was, in recent weeks, an outspoken opponent of the plans to develop Lawrence House into a private health spa. He delivered a speech at the recent public enquiry and gathered considerable local support, but the buildings committee of the council subsequently met and voted in favour of the spa development.

Councilor Aubrey Pike, leader of the council, offered this tribute today: "Peter Sloan will be sadly missed by myself and all members of the council, whatever their political affiliation. He and I did not always see eye to eye, but he was a worthy opponent. We are all horrified at this terrible, outrageous crime and appeal to any who may be able to assist the police with their enquiries to step forward immediately.

"Finally, we would like to say that this is even more tragic because our crime rates are so low in Frenton. Future visitors and tourists may come here knowing that a warm, safe welcome awaits them."

Police request that any witnesses should contact them immediately on 02243 777777, and assure the public that all responses will be treated in confidence.

He's dead. He's dead. And I didn't even know for hours. Sick.

Forgot to charge my cell phone, so didn't get the news the night it happened, but Mum had decided not to call me anyway until I had done the marathon.

"Your dad would have wanted you to run that race," she said, "because of all the training you had done and the money you were raising."

So it wasn't until I borrowed James's cell on the way home to tell my parents about my run that Mum could blurt out the terrible news. When I got to the house, the police were there. Mum kept breaking down. There are no suspects. Forensics say they'd slashed into my dad thirteen times. Thirteen. James had to identify the body. I couldn't.

When I went out today, people acted as if nothing had happened. They bought food and went to the bank and read newspapers. Nothing had changed. For them.

Just when I thought things couldn't get any worse, I had to go and see Hayley today. I got a couple of days off for compassionate leave, but the funeral has been delayed because of forensics and the post-mortem report is still pending and I was going mad anyway. I am so bitter I can taste it. And the grind goes on.

Anyway, I went back to work. I went to Hayley's house.

"I heard about your dad," she said, matter-of-factly. For a moment, I thought that she was going to say something kind, something comforting—that would have been the obvious thing.

"So now you know how it feels, miss. You took my dad

away from me. Now you've lost yours. How do you like it, eh?"

I wanted to wipe that grinning, evil sneer off her face. And perhaps that's what she was looking for—a slap that would have cost me my job, and then I'd have lost my career as well as my father. I couldn't speak; she stunned me into silence.

Enough. Must sleep now.

Tuesday, September 13

I hate. It's ironic, really. I hate because I loved. I can't stop hating those teenagers who did that to my father.

James and Vanessa and Katy have taken over the running of the youth club. To think one of those kids might have even been there, might have even joined in ... They might even know who did it. I want to beat them all senseless until they tell me the truth. I want justice. No, I don't. I want to hurt the scum who did this to my dad.

Wednesday, September 14

I tried on my black dress and then realized that my black dress made my cleavage look more "come and get me boys" than "my father has been stabbed to death by a gang of unidentified youths on whom I wish to perpetrate vigilante violence." Do you even have to wear black to funerals these days? Will people think I don't love my father enough if I don't wear black? Am I allowed to wear makeup? Blow-dry my hair?

I have called my mother. She is wearing her electric blue Jackie-O suit. She said it was one of my Dad's favorite things—he loved her wearing it. I have decided on black trousers, white shirt with purple cardigan and flat shoes.

Friday, September 16

The funeral was yesterday. My father is dead and nothing can change that.

My crying now sounds inhuman to me. And I can't stop. Which others say to expect. But odd things make me feel like I'm going mad ... like hearing Dad in the next room or thinking I saw him catching a bus last week—he never caught buses, for goodness' sake—or feeling sick or shouting at the television or having a huge email argument with a colleague and copying in the entire office by accident or wanting to push the police out of the way so I could do their job ...

There are no stages of grief—just a series of states, each one worse than the last. Anger ... guilt (why wasn't I there to protect him?) ... the "if onlys" ... and the pain. I never knew that grief could actually be a physical pain, and painkillers don't touch it. Alcohol numbs it, but then I feel worse the next day.

The funeral was held at the little church my parents went to in the village. There were even people crammed in the vestry. Everybody from my church was there. The vicar seemed nice in a distant, bumbling sort of way, but before the funeral he visited my parents' cottage and asked us if we would like to choose any particular hymns or readings.

If only this terrible heartache would stop. I can't pray. I guess I blame God for what happened, for I have nothing to say to him.

During the funeral my dad's coffin was displayed at the front, and I couldn't stop imagining him lying in there. Then I looked around at the church that was supposed to be about life and resurrection, and yet there was this dead man in that coffin—my lovely kind smiling dead dad. Dead. I wanted Dad to sit up. And I wanted those who murdered him to take his place lying down.

After a hymn my mother went to the front and spoke about my father a little bit. She told everybody how they had met in a university library, and she pretended to be a student too so he wouldn't think she was stupid. She was actually working at the local pub at the time. She talked of God and how much Jesus was helping her through. This gave me mixed feelings. I was so glad my mother was finding some love and support somewhere, but I felt cheated. By God. I felt no comfort.

After the funeral everyone went into a room at the back of the church and nervously picked at the food my mother and I had prepared—everyone apart from the vicar, who was wolfing down half a plate of cucumber sandwiches that he later congratulated my mother on. It's weird to watch people dealing with death in different ways. Some nervously try to avoid your gaze because they know that they can't bring anyone back to life and therefore can't make it better, and some babble on about the traffic and, well, the cucumber sandwiches. I hate cucumber sandwiches.

My mother was talking to Robert and Nola when suddenly Mr. and Mrs. Hemming bustled up to them. It was then I got a horrible feeling in my stomach. I heard Mr. Hemming tell my mother that it had been an "interesting" funeral. Mr. Hemming continued.

"You know, Kitty, is it? It's hard to lose a loved one, but we must remember that God is sovereign, and if he chooses to take someone away, we must accept that it is his will and get on with things."

My mother gave him a look. I know that look. It's a warning. Carry on at your peril. I've seen it on my mother's face before—only once or twice, but I'd recognize it anywhere.

Mr. Hemming was obviously unaware that he was now in mortal peril, so he blabbered on. "The Lord decided that your husband should suffer this fate, for one reason or another. He is in charge. We thank him even though we don't understand, convinced that ultimately his will has been done."

With this my mother drew back her hand and slapped Mr. Hemming's face so hard that he actually rocked on his feet and had to clutch onto Mrs. Hemming for support.

He yelled and then turned to Robert, who had moved in closer, sensing trouble at the same time as I did.

Mr. Hemming almost shouted at Robert. "I think we need to pray for this woman. She is obviously mad with grief."

Robert stared at Mr. Hemming, his nostrils flared with anger. He said nothing.

"Robert!" Mrs. Hemming barked. "Answer my husband! He is a deacon in your church, and he's just been assaulted!"

Robert carried on staring at him, and I noticed he was breathing heavily. Nola had by now put her hand on his arm and was looking worried.

At last Robert spoke, softly and slowly. "No," he said and paused. And then he turned to my mum. "Kitty, I am so sorry for what has happened here."

"Rebuke that woman!" screamed Mrs. Hemming. "We demand you rebuke that woman!"

Mr. Hemming was going redder and redder in the face. Then he drew himself up stiffly and announced "My wife is right. If you do not rebuke that woman, then I'll ... I'll ... I'll resign!"

Robert said nothing. The silence grew and grew.

And that was that. They both stomped out without another word.

So the funeral had its plusses. The Hemmings have finally left New Wave Christian Fellowship. Perhaps it's unkind of me to be happy about that, but frankly my father has been stabbed to death and I'll search for any kind of happiness I can get.

Robert says the Hemmings are still welcome, but only if they refrain from handing out any of their un-Christlike advice.

My mother says that she felt much better after hitting someone and that she wished Mr. Hemming would come back and say something else stupid so that she could slap him again.

Nola says that if Mum hadn't slapped him, Robert probably would have and then he would have been the one losing his position, not Mr. Hemming.

But then the funeral had its minuses. And they came in the form of a secret I really didn't want to know. I had gone outside the church for some fresh air when I noticed a figure half-hiding behind a tree. I peered at it, wondering who it was, and I realized it was Aaron. He looked a mess. He had a black eye—actually more like a black eye, black cheek, and black lip. He appeared to have been crying. A lot.

In fact, he looked like he had been crying more than I had. I'm sure he was also drunk; in fact, he looked like he had mugged a homeless alcoholic for his clothes and then gone out and got drunk.

"Aaron. What's the matter?" I asked.

"I'm sorry," he blurted out. "I'm really so sorry …"

"You look more upset than I do," I replied. "You almost look like it was your dad who died."

With this, he bent over double and groaned, as though I'd hit him hard in the stomach.

"For goodness sake, Aaron. I really don't want to hear about your problems right now. There's a room full of people in there who are all trying to be nice to me. And in a minute I've got to pretend that I can hold a normal conversation without wanting to cry so hard I stop breathing, and you're out here, drunk and being crazy, as usual. I don't think I can deal with you right now."

He looked up at me, his eyes swollen red, and slurred "Helen, look, I need to tell you something. I don't think I'm supposed to because of the police investigation and everything, but I thought you should know ..."

"Police investigation? What police investigation?" For the moment I thought that he'd been arrested for drugs or something and now was showing up here to whine to me about his stupidity ...

"Helen. It was me. I was the guy those kids were attacking when your father stopped his car. I managed to get away as he was talking to them. I thought he'd be okay. I thought he could just get into his car and drive away if they got violent. So I ran into the pub to call the police. When I got back, they had gone, and your dad was lying there, lying there like a doll or something. At first I didn't even think he was real. He was unconscious, losing so much blood. I held him, Helen, I want you to know that. He didn't die by himself. I should have stayed. I should have protected him. I'm so sorry. But I did hold him and his blood soaked into my clothes and got into my hair and I held him and I didn't let go. Not till a long time after he was gone, just in case. I know that changes nothing, Helen, but it's the only thing I have."

And that was that. He stared at me for a while, eyes wide, pleading, then stumbled away. I tried to call after him but he didn't seem to hear. I didn't even know what I was going to say. Part of me—part of me—feels so sorry for him. But part of me—part of me—thinks I would prefer for him to be dead right now, if that meant that my father would still be alive. If I could swap their lives, I'd do it in a blink of an eye. I'd do it right now.

Friday, September 23

Nothing has changed since the funeral. I decided not to try to track Aaron down. This week's newspaper reports an interesting story:

> Tension is rising this week in the City Council as the national media increase their pressure on party leader David Howard over the Peter Sloane murder. Sloane, a local councilor in Frenton, was campaigning over the sale of Lawrence House, a council-owned building. Questions have arisen over the intended sale of the building, and a source who asked not to be identified, has confirmed that it has come to light that the wife of the councilor behind the decision, Councilor Aubrey Pike, 56, is the sister of James Burton, 45, the businessman who intended to purchase the property. Burton is a property magnate whose chain of exclusive health spas can be found in almost every major city in the country.
>
> A family man, Sloane leaves wife, Kitty, 54, daughter, Helen, 27.

The council has invited me to move the youth club to Lawrence House. Apparently they have finally caved in to public opinion and want to dedicate the whole building to the local community, with services for all ages—babies, children, youth—all through to the old. It would mean much better facilities, everything we wanted.

And I couldn't care less. I'm the last person who should be allowed to look after young people. I have violent fantasies about what I would do to them (well, a certain group of them, if I ever tracked them down).

I saw Hayley yesterday, and I didn't hate her as much as usual. But if my feelings don't change significantly, I'm going to have to give up my job. Being a social worker and working with young people is the only thing I ever wanted to do. I know so much about Hayley's life now, though I wish I knew more. What if her next social worker didn't do their job properly? What would happen to her? What will happen to her anyway?

I called mother, and she dodged questions about what I should do. She told me to try to think about what my father would say. Then I phoned Nola and asked her to come by.

Nola came round and wanted to listen (mostly), talk (a little), and pray. I feel a little better. I think I am finding it hard to pray because I'm still so angry inside—not just at God, but at the whole world, at whoever it was who murdered my father. And I'm mad at everybody else for not protecting him.

A glimmer of hope did appear today from somewhere. The rage is still with me. I don't even know if I want it to leave. But I have decided to go ahead with the youth club move. I've asked James, Vanessa, Nola, and Robert to help me and pray for me.

I'm not any better, but I'm too tired to feel anything much. Working so hard means I collapse into bed exhausted at night and I don't have to dwell on what happened to Dad. There are all sorts of admin things to do to get ready to move the youth club to its new venue, even though it isn't ready yet and won't be for some time. I hate paperwork ...

We are going to have a memorial service for Dad in a week or so. It was Councilor Pike's idea. I still don't find him easy to like, but he came to Mum and said he thought it would be a wonderful way of celebrating Dad's life. All the councilors are coming—those he fought with and those he fought alongside. I guess it is Pike's way of saying he's sorry. It means more planning, more ideas.

Saturday, October 29

The memorial service was quite an event. As I sit on my bed now, writing this, I feel okay. Sort of. The pain of my father's death is still like a stab in my heart. But I'm a little happier, I think. A different, more complicated type of happiness than I'm used to, but happier nonetheless.

We held the service in the church, because it could accommodate all the people, and asked Robert to do a short talk at the end, explaining a little bit about my father's faith. I believe that my father's death was totally meaningless and unplanned—but if God can use it in the slightest way for good, than I want him to. God wasn't the architect of his death, but perhaps he can be the redeemer of it. At least I want to believe that. My father used his life for good, and I think he would have wanted his death used for good as well. And lots of councilors and people he had worked with and neighbors and friends—they all wanted to be able to say something about what Dad had meant to them. We had to limit them in the end, or the service would have gone on for hours.

It seemed like half the town showed up. Aaron came too. I noticed him standing at the back. All the councilors, everybody was there. It was horribly sad and yet comforting at the same time—how can something be so bittersweet? Robert spoke with the warmth and kindness that makes us all love him so much.

"Peter Sloane was a good man, but Peter Sloane was also a Christian man. Sadly, those are two statements that don't necessarily go hand in hand. But Peter understood what it was to be a true Christian, to be the kind of person that Jesus was. Peter was a man who hated corruption and loved his community. Like Jesus, Peter's vision was to try to look after those who have nowhere else to go and to care about those who don't have the opportunities that many others enjoy. So he would have been overjoyed that Lawrence House will, in time, become the Peter Sloane Community Centre — dedicated to the people he cared about. People mattered to him; it is no exaggeration to say Peter literally gave up his life so that another person might live. He went to the aid of a young man under attack, and it cost Peter his life.

"If there is a prayer in your heart for Christ or for the new community centre, then I'd like to invite you, as a symbol of that prayer, to come up here and light a candle and place it on the table behind me."

Almost at once people started coming forward. I think Robert and Nola must have used up Ikea's entire supply of night lights. After lighting mine, I was about to walk forward when I turned and caught Aaron's eye. He had moved to stand a little closer to me, and now he was shyly picking his way to the front. He looked up, and as he saw me, he looked worried and wavered, as if he was going to turn back. By now his bruises had faded, and he was back in his usual garb of black polo neck and skinny jeans. He looked tired. I smiled at him and nodded, as if to say, go on, it's all right, go ahead. He nodded nervously back.

Suddenly, someone flicked a switch and turned the lights off. Once again Aaron and I found ourselves staring at each other in the candlelight, just like we had in the poetry café, a lifetime ago. Strangely, I don't think that either of us wanted to be the first one to look away. I remembered how we had spun around those lampposts, how everything was so much easier back then, even though I didn't realize it. I wanted to turn back time and be with him again in those moments, without any other thought in the world.

And yet because of him my father was dead.

He looked so much better than the last time I'd seen him. He made his way up to the table and placed his lit candle on it, came back down again, and slipped into the back of the crowd. I watched him go, feeling confused, knowing it might be a very long time before I could speak to him again. And then I walked slowly toward the table, flickering candle in hand. Suddenly I notice that Vanessa and James and Nola were beside me. Nola put her arms around my shoulders. I couldn't hold back the tears as I looked at the dozens of flickering lights that covered the table. I placed mine down.

"Thanks, lovely Dad. I miss you and I hate it that you're not here. But if God will stick with me, I think I could be strong," I whispered.

I dabbed my eyes with a tissue and went back to sit down again. Vanessa, James, and Nola went back to their seats. And it was then that I noticed Laura sitting a couple of seats down from me with her eyes closed. She must have sensed someone looking at her—she opened her eyes and looked at me.

"Just thought I'd try praying how Vanessa prays," she said, "though without the dancing, of course."

I suddenly got the giggles, remembering Vanessa stalking round Laura's garden, killing her plants with communion wine.

"What?" Laura asked, giggling herself now. "What's so funny?"

"Nothing," I replied. "Just thinking about Vanessa and her craziness. I like it sometimes, to be honest."

"Me too," said Laura. "I've never known anyone so passionate about God and all that Christian stuff before. We all know she's a bit barmy, and yet there's something solid there, buried deep in her, and whenever I'm with her, you know, I feel completely safe. Like she loves me. I don't know why, but that makes me want to pray."

"I know exactly what you mean," I replied.

And then suddenly, someone somewhere flicked the lights back on, and I got the shock of my life. Hayley had come. She was leaning against a pillar, wearing a tracksuit and gold earrings so big you could have used them for hula hoops. Her hair was scraped so far back off her temples she looked like she'd had an overenthusiastic facelift. She looked up, caught my eye, and gave me the usual scowl before returning her glare to the floor. I couldn't believe it. She shows up at my father's memorial service and she's still the same sulky adolescent mess.

Then she turned and looked across at me again and

then back down immediately, awkward and uncomfortable. Which is no wonder, considering all her hideous jibes. I felt like walking right over there and kicking her out. I wasn't going to allow her to ruin this.

But then, after looking down for a second or two, her head came up once again and her eyes met mine. I decided to try. I waved and nodded a hello, still expecting that she might return the compliment with a one-fingered signal or a sneer. But she raised her hand, waved back, and mouthed, "Hi, Helen ..."

It was then that I saw it, on Hayley's face. It was so fleeting I could have missed it. But I saw it. It was the slightest hint, like sunshine peering for a second from behind a cloud, of a smile.

For news of Jeff Lucas's ministry, to access his blog, or to purchase resources, visit www.jefflucas.org.

Acknowledgments

Writing as a twenty-seven-year-old woman is a new experience for me! This book would not have been possible without the talents of Tamsin Kendrick, who is a gifted writer and poet. She not only allowed me to peer into the mysterious space which is the twenty-something female Christian mind, but helped greatly with ideas, plot twists, character color, and words. And she came to Eastbourne in the UK and also Colorado to help make this book happen. Eastbourne is lovely, but I think she preferred Colorado ... Thanks, Tamsin.

My thanks to my daughter, Kelly, my favorite social worker in the universe. Kelly is nothing like Helen, but shares the same profession: her insights were invaluable.

Chris and Jeanne, thanks for the beach house—the perfect place to finish a book ... and thanks for our wonderful friendship.

And Kay, you smiled and were unfailingly kind and understanding during the mad writing time. You've been smiling in my direction for quite some time now. I love you for it.

Share Your Thoughts

With the Author: Your comments will be forwarded to the author when you send them to *zauthor@zondervan.com*.

With Zondervan: Submit your review of this book by writing to *zreview@zondervan.com*.

Free Online Resources at
www.zondervan.com

Zondervan AuthorTracker: Be notified whenever your favorite authors publish new books, go on tour, or post an update about what's happening in their lives at www.zondervan.com/authortracker.

Daily Bible Verses and Devotions: Enrich your life with daily Bible verses or devotions that help you start every morning focused on God. Visit www.zondervan.com/newsletters.

Free Email Publications: Sign up for newsletters on Christian living, academic resources, church ministry, fiction, children's resources, and more. Visit www.zondervan.com/newsletters.

Zondervan Bible Search: Find and compare Bible passages in a variety of translations at www.zondervanbiblesearch.com.

Other Benefits: Register to receive online benefits like coupons and special offers, or to participate in research.

ZONDERVAN.com/
AUTHORTRACKER
follow your favorite authors